*Hannah's Huggers - Building Gods
Army of Love*

Hannah's Huggers - Building Gods Army of Love

Building Gods Army of Love

Andy Smith

TKR Publishing
Nashville, TN

Contents

DEDICATION

I dedicate this book to the four friends of the Smith family
whose names I used for the four children recruited by
Hannah.
One (Cindy) has passed away from cancer,
the other three (Erica, Jerry and Lauren)
continue to fight for their lives because of cancer.
As my daughter, Tracy who passed away from breast
cancer in 2013, would often say,
"BE BRAVE!"

Disclaimer

"Oh come on, Chris! Are you going to show up in my living room every time I finish a book?"

Chris just sits comfortably in my recliner with a smile on his face.

"Listen, I haven't even published this book yet, but when I do, I'm going to publish it as fiction, so you better get use to it." I tell my guardian angel who once again has that annoying smile on his face.

"God is not smiling, my friend … he's not smiling." says Chris with a cautionary tone.

"Listen Chris, we had this discussion when I finished *Johnny's Story*, and nothing has changed with this one. I have rules I have to go with and no matter what you say, Hannah's Huggers is going to be published as a fiction, not a non-fiction, so save your breath."

"Have you read the Bible?"

"Well for the most part."

"And is it considered fiction, or non-fiction?" Chris says with that smile.

"Well I suppose it's a non-fiction."

Chris smiles and nods, "You suppose correctly, my friend." he pauses and looks at me with a smug expression that I could seriously do without, "And have you ever read the book of Revelations in this non-fiction Bible?"

"That's different, Chris. A lot of people have read Revelations without any clue of what the hell John was talking about."

"Exactly! Yet some fools on some committee 1500 years ago decided to put that in the 'non-fiction' Bible and now you have a handful of idiots running around the world making millions of dollars telling people how the world is going to end because they're so smart and have figured Revelations out."

"Well I wasn't on that committee, pal, and if I was, I would have screamed at the notion that Revelations was non-fiction. Nobody knows what that book's about!"

"Do you know that is the number one question people ask when they come over to this side? I'm telling you John is one frustrated saint because God tells us angels to just send them to John – he wrote it, he can explain it."

"Well I'm sorry for John. Maybe he should have picked a better cave to hang out in. But We have to work something out here Chris, because I don't want God getting upset every time I write a story and publish it as fiction. No matter how much you convince me that it's all true, I just can't go non-fiction with these stories."

Chris looks at me with a much more polite smile, "Look

Andy, we understand the world you live in now. God gets it. I didn't come here to argue with you or tell you how to publish your stories. God loves your work and he wanted me to tell you that there are many more stories in the Bible that need to be told."

Chris pauses and I hesitate on how agreeable his tone is as he continues, "God really gets frustrated because the Bible just gives people a small bite of what happened. He really wanted someone to elaborate on the Samaritan at the well story, because there was so much more to say. They mention it, say Jesus spent a couple of days in their village and then just skip over to another story. They totally missed Hannah. They totally missed the source of Paul's 1Corinthians13 chapter of Love. God is so pleased that because of you, Hannah is finally getting recognition that she so richly deserves. It's frustrating to see you get recognition as a creative fiction writer because it diminishes Hannah's story as simply a cute story you made up, you can understand that, right."

As usual, Chris always makes a good point.

"I do understand, Chris. I'm sorry Hannah's story will get recognized as a cute story I made up and not recognized as a true story of a great woman. As a writer, I do understand how many of the twists and turns in my stories just came to me out of the blue and I really don't have a problem in recognizing that when these ideas pop into my head, it's God leading me down the path that he wants the story to go. I get that. It really is humbling when I finish a story like this and read through it and realize how lucky I am to have had this story just drop into my lap. That's why I don't have a problem believing that these stories do come from God. I'm not that clever, I know that. I don't do any research. If these stories come from God as you say, I can only say 'Thank You'. I love telling these stories and I hope they are true. They need to be true."

I need a break, "Look, I promise to write a disclaimer every time I have a story that comes like *7Days, Johnny's Story* or *Hannah's Huggers*. I would love to write more stories for God and will always leave my heart open to his direction. But it has to be published as fiction."

"I know, my friend, and God knows it too. If the writers of the Bible stories had to deal with the rules of publishing like you do nowadays, the Bible would have been a pamphlet at best."

Chris smiles and once again we both seem satisfied with the results of our talk. I know I say a lot of bad things about my guardian angel, but truth be told, he really has been a big help to me.

"I'll tell you what I'll do, Smitty boy. There's no need for me to come here after every book you write. As long as you understand that there are many great untold stories in the Bible, that God would love to see you explore. So from now on, the only time I'll come here is when you write something God wants no part of. You'll be on your own in that case. So if I'm not here when you finish a story, slap a disclaimer in the beginning and we'll be okay. If you just make stuff up that God wants no part of, I'll be here to make sure you don't put in a disclaimer. Got it?"

"Got it."

Chris smiles at me annoyingly again, "Now do you want me to have Hannah send you someone to give you a hug?" he says as he bats his eyes at me.

"Let's leave the children out of this. I'm afraid if a girl gives me a hug and whispers, 'Think Non-Fiction' in my ear, I don't care how cute she might be, we will have a problem."

"Okay buddy-pal … Again, God wanted me to thank you for telling Hannah's story. You do nice work."

With that, Chris is gone and I realize it's after midnight and I'm beat.

READER BEWARE:
THIS BOOK IS PUBLISHED AS FICTION
BY PUBLISHING RULES THAT
PUBLISHED REVELATIONS IN THE BIBLE AS
NON-FICTION.
IN BOTH CASES, YOU ARE ON YOUR OWN!....

author

Part I

The Samaritan Woman

1

Living Water

"May I have a drink of your water?"

Ruth chuckles to herself, "How is it that you, being a Jewish man, should ask me, a Samaritan woman for a drink of water?"

"If you knew who it was asking you for a drink of water, you would ask him and he would give you a drink of the living water."

Ruth is curios. This was not a normal Jewish man. A Jewish man would rather suffer from thirst than have any words with the lowly Samaritan woman.

"This well is deep, and you have no rope or anything to draw out the water, so how could you give me this living water you speak of? Are you greater than Jacob, who gave us this well?"

"Whoever drinks from this well becomes thirsty again and comes back over and over again for more. The living water which I give does not come from such a well. It bubbles up like a continual spring within, and that person never grows thirsty again."

Ruth laughs, but is intrigued by this man's words.

"Well I want that kind of water so that I will not need to return and refill my water-jug in this tiresome way."

He smiles at Ruth and is also intrigued at the confidence this woman has in talking with him.

"Go get your husband and come back and I will tell you more about this living water."

Ruth looks at him and doesn't hesitate, "I have no husband."

He smiles at her.

"You are an honest woman. The man who lives with you is not your husband." He continues to point out other issues of Ruth's past that only a few people would know.

Ruth is taken back. How can this complete stranger – a Jewish man no less- know so much about her life?

"You must be a prophet!" is her only response to what he has said, " You Jews worship God in Jerusalem, yet we worship God in Samaria. You tell me where we should worship God, then."

"God brought salvation through the Jews, but the time has come when people do not need to go to Jerusalem, nor Samaria to worship God, for God is a spirit and not found in any one place. Those who worship God the right way must worship him in spirit."

Ruth looks at this man who speaks unlike any other man she has spoken to.

"I know the Messiah is coming from God, and when he comes he will tell us everything."

He smiles at her, "I am he that you are waiting for."

Ruth looks at him with a strong sense of understanding that this truly is the one sent by God.

Before she can continue the conversation, she sees his disciples coming up the road and knows it would be best if she leaves now. She doesn't take her jug of water as she hurries off to go back to her village to tell everyone about this man who knew everything that she had done in her past. Many follow Ruth back to the well, where he is talking with his disciples.

The Samaritans wanted to find out who this man was. As they approached the well, his disciples became very uncomfortable and concerned.

"Why don't you head to Galilee and I'll follow up behind you?"

The disciples didn't ask any question as they immediately left him for Galilee. They had learned not to ask him too many questions in situations like this even though they were extremely curios as to why he was willing to stay behind and talk to these people a Jewish man would never speak to.

As his disciples leave, the Samaritans gather at the well and start questioning him.

"How is it that a Jewish man as yourself would know everything about this Samaritan woman's past?"

"A good father knows everything about his children."

"What gives you authority to refer to this woman as your child? You are a Jew and Jews despise the Samaritans."

"I am from my father. I was sent to tell everyone who will listen that we are all God's children and his love is unconditional."

They look at one another confused and wondering if this just might be the Messiah they have been told would come.

"Are you truly the Messiah that we have been told would come?"

"I am." he smiles.

They are all speechless as this man speaks so confidently and with such authority. He must be the Messiah as only a fool would say this if it were not so.

Ruth speaks up, "Maybe you could come with us to our village and speak to us more about God's love?"

"I'd love to." he says, as Ruth doesn't hesitate to turn and start leading them all back to the village.

As they head down the rocky road, a man questions him.

"Are you not concerned of your people seeing you walking and talking with us?"

"My people are not of this world. I am not the least bit concerned of the teachings and traditions of this world. My only concern is the message of God's eternal love for all people."

At this, the people look at one another in amazement. They had never heard a man speak in such a manner.

~~~~~~~~~~

Jesus spent two days in the small village, helping others
~~~~~~~~~~

with chores and answering any and all questions they had. As evening fell, Jesus was invited to sit in the main gathering place of the village and tell the Samaritans more about God. The Samaritans were not only amazed at how open he was and willing to speak to them, but the message he spoke was unlike any other they had ever heard before.

These were people who were despised by the Jews and the Romans, so they had learned to stay pretty much to themselves and quietly live in their villages without drawing a lot of attention from the outside world. The message Jesus spoke to them was about things these people had never heard about before. Love was the main topic, but he also talked about faith, caring, feeling compassion, being kind to your neighbors. These were things no one ever talked about before. They lived in a world that simply did chores, paid taxes and followed whatever rules that were required in order to have peace. This man was teaching them to look at life in a totally different perspective.

He truly must be from God.

While visiting the Samaritans, he befriended a little girl named Hannah. She was the daughter of Ruth. About eight years old, she was a very curios girl who asked Jesus a million questions. Jesus seemed to delight in his conversations with Hannah and was never in a hurry to cut them short. She asked a lot of questions and Jesus was always happy to respond.

Hannah lived pretty much alone with her mother. Ruth was not a favored woman in the village, as the man she lived with was always gone and only dropped in from time to time when he was in the area. Everyone knew that he was not the father of Hannah. So Hannah lived a fairly quite life with her mother, both being tolerated in the village and for the most part outcasts in their world.

Ruth was a strong woman who understood her place in society, but never complained. She was especially interested in what Jesus was talking about because from her perspective, there was so much about her life missing. She felt that nobody loved her and that most of the villagers didn't make much of an effort to engage with her or her daughter. Yet her heart was strong and she was determined to make the most of her life and the life of her little girl. That's why Ruth was so willing to talk with Jesus at the well. She understood that she was pretty much at the bottom of the social ladder of life, so she had nothing to lose by challenging this Jewish stranger who asked her for a drink of water.

Jesus saw a lot of strength in Ruth and felt that it was people like her that God sent him to reach out to the most. The forgotten people that society simply tossed away for whatever reasons. He could see in her a good heart and was especially attentive while he stayed in the village to her and her little girl.

"Have you ever met God?" asked Hannah when she had a moment alone with Jesus.

"I have."

"What's he like?" she continues.

"God is love …. God is a spirit."

"How do you know you've met him?" asks Hannah, unsure of what Jesus means by 'spirit'.

"I see him in your smile. I hear him in the chirping birds. I feel him when I splash the cool waters of the river on my hot face."

Hannah looks even more confused, but is not willing to give up. "How do you know it is God?"

Jesus smiles as he loves the innocence of the children he speaks to. "Because God is love, so every time I see, hear or feel something that brings love into my heart, I know it is God being with me."

"I don't think I understand love. I've never heard anyone talk about it." says Hannah with complete confusion in her face.

"Love is patient and kind. When you are kind to others, not because you have to be, but because you want others to be happy, that is love."

Hannah thinks about it before she continues, "But I don't see very many happy people."

"That's why God has sent me to this village. People spend their days doing chores and works because they simply want to live in peace and not get into trouble, right?"

"I guess so."

"But when you do chores for your mother, do you do it because you want to stay out of trouble?"

"No. I want my mother to be happy, so I help her out."

"Exactly! It's not about doing chores, it's about the why.

Why do you do the chores? Too many people do chores to stay out of trouble and as you know, they are not very happy people, are they?"

"They don't seem to be."

"But I have come to tell them if they do chores like you do for your mother, to make her happy, they are doing chores from a heart of love and that's what pleases God."

"Don't people want to make others happy?"

"I think they do, Hannah. That's why I'm here. I think most people worry too much about doing chores to stay out of trouble when they need to understand that if they do chores to help each other out and make people happy, like you do for your mother, they will find the best way to stay out of trouble."

"It sounds simple, but do you think they will listen to you?"

"Oh, it's up to people to listen or not. I'll have to leave tomorrow to catch up with the others, but maybe you could help me out."

Hannah brightens, "Sure."

"After I leave, maybe you could make it your chore to make God happy by giving everyone in the village a hug when you see them."

"Oh I'm not sure many people around here would want me to hug them." Hannah says with a scary face.

Jesus smiles, "No doubt, young lady. But at least you know your mother would love it, right?"

Hannah brightens, "I think so."

"Of course she would. So every morning when you wake up, you start your day by going to your mother and give her a big hug and say, "Hope you have a good day mother" and I promise you that will start her day off in a very happy way."

"I promise, I'll do that."

"And then when you're out in the village, you can ask the people you pass if you can give them a hug. Most will scurry away from you because they have no idea how great a nice hug is, but if you keep asking, someone is going to say 'yes'. Just give them a nice hug like you do your mother and tell them 'I hope you're having a good day' and before long, everyone in the village is going to be looking for the little girl who gives them hugs and makes them happy. In time, you will look around your village and see happy people doing chores, not because they want to stay out of trouble, but because they want to make others happy and live in a village full of happy people. And that's how you make God happy, Hannah. God loves happy people."

Hannah smiles, "That would be great!"

"You want to practice?" says Jesus.

Hannah smiles, "Okay."

Jesus gets up and walks away from Hannah about ten steps before turning around. He stands up straight, folds his arms and puts on a grumpy, stern face.

"Okay, pretend I'm one of the grumpy old men of the village. My name is Mr. Grump. When you come by, ask me if I want a hug, okay?"

Hannah laughs and says "Okay"

Hannah starts to walk until she gets to Jesus and stops, "Hi, Mr. Grump (she giggles), would you like a hug?"

Jesus looks down at her sternly and says, "I would NOT!", then looks away.

Then Jesus looks down at Hannah and smiles, "You'll probably hear that a lot, but it's okay. Just say, 'Okay, Mr. Grump. Have a nice day' and move on. But remember not to call everyone Mr. Grump, got it?"

Hannah laughs, "Okay. Got it."

"Now let's try it again, only this time I'll be one of the town women named Miss Grump, okay?"

"Okay." says Hannah as she skips back to her starting place and turns around.

Jesus stands up straight again with a stern look and says, "Okay."

Hannah starts to walk towards Jesus then stops again and asks, "Hi, Miss Grump (she giggles again), would you like a hug?"

Jesus looks down at Hannah with a stern face but seems to be considering the option. Then he(she) looks around as if to be seeing if anyone is watching her, then back at Hannah. "I suppose, little girl, if you must." he(she) says as he(she) looks away, then looks down at Hannah and smiles, "This is when you walk up to her and give her a nice hug as you do your mother, then step back and say, 'Have a nice day.' and move on, got it?"

"Got it," she giggles as Jesus stands up straight again.

Hannah gives him a big hug, steps back and says, "Have a nice day." and moves on.

Immediately, Jesus starts clapping his hands in approval and gets down on one knee as Hannah comes running to him and gives him a big hug, then steps back.

"Well done, Hannah," says Jesus as they make their way back to where they began.

"At first, you won't get a lot of hugs, but don't be discouraged, okay? God's love is in your heart and as long as God is in your heart, things well get better."

"Maybe they'll talk to my mother again?"

Jesus sits again on the wall and pulls Hannah onto his lap and looks at her with soft compassion.

"I know that it's been hard for you and your mother. It seems like nobody around here likes you, right?"

Hannah nods to confirm as Jesus continues.

"Well most people have trouble forgiving others of their mistakes. But God does. God's love is unconditional. Do you know what that means, Hannah?"

Hannah shakes her head no.

"It's like I was saying earlier how people do chores to stay out of trouble, but everybody makes mistakes. Everybody makes bad choices. What people need to learn is that you can't correct your mistakes by doing more chores and obeying more rules. You correct your mistakes by understanding that Gods love will always forgive you no matter what mistakes you make. That's what unconditional love is, Hannah. Your mother has made some mistakes in her past that most of the others seem to hold against her. They don't have to forgive her, but she needs to understand that God will forgive her if she just admits she did wrong and says 'I'm sorry' to God in her heart. We all make mistakes, Hannah, and it's important to understand that if you pray to God and say you're sorry, God will always forgive you and continue to love you. Gods love never fails."

Hannah smiles and gives Jesus a big hug as Jesus see Ruth coming back from her daily trip to the well.

"Here comes your mother. Why don't you go give her a big hug just like we practiced." Jesus says as Hannah jumps off of his lap and runs over to her mother.

As Ruth and Hannah come into the village, Ruth stops to thank Jesus for watching her while she was away.

"I hope she didn't bother you too much. She doesn't have a lot of friends to play with or talk to, so she normally just stays in our home and plays by herself."

Jesus smiles, "Hannah was no trouble at all. She's a very engaging young girl. You're a good mother, Ruth."

Ruth scoffs at the compliment, "Well I guess I've done one thing right I suppose." as she looks down at her daughter and smiles.

"You've done a lot of things right, Ruth. God judges us by our heart, and you have a very good heart, Ruth."

"Well I'm pretty sure most of the people around here would disagree with you, Jesus."

Jesus smiles, "I wouldn't worry about them, Ruth. They make mistakes, too. And they think that by doing tasks and performing sacrifices, that they are getting right with God, but that's not how it works. They may or may not forgive you of your past sins, but that's up to them and their hearts. What's important is that you forgive yourself by understanding that Gods love is in your heart and that love is unconditional. Getting right with God means being a loving person to everyone, especially those who speak against you."

Ruth looks at Jesus with a smile, "You must be the Messiah as I have never heard anyone speak of love as you have."

Jesus stands and gives Ruth a nice hug, then steps away. "I learned to hug from Hannah," Jesus smiles, "She gives really good hugs. I'm guessing Hannah's hugs could probably soften a lot of stuffy hearts around here."

Ruth looks down at Hannah, "Well I, for one, would never refuse a hug from this girl." as Hannah embraces her mother, and Jesus winks at Hannah.

"Jesus and I practiced it today. He pretended to be Mr. Grump and Miss Grump. It was fun!"

Jesus laughs, "Now don't you get me in trouble young lady. Remember, these people have names, so no Mr. Grump or Miss Grump, okay?"

Hannah laughs, "Don't worry, I'll be nice to them."

Ruth looks at her daughter, then to Jesus. "I'm sure glad I ran into you at the well. You've given me hope, which I haven't felt in a long time. Thank you."

Jesus smiles, "God's love is the only hope you need, and always available to every open heart. I've enjoyed my stay here and appreciate everyone letting me share God's love and message. I need to leave in the morning and catch up to my brothers. Who would have thought that a mighty Jew as I would truly enjoy the fellowship of the lowly Samaritans of this village, right?"

Ruth laughs with Jesus, "Only the true Messiah could have pulled that off for sure."

That evening, the villagers were gathered in the square to listen to Jesus more. Many of the villagers believed him and were amazed at his message of love.

Ruth and Hannah stayed on the outer edge and pretty much stayed quiet, understanding their position within their community.

But Hannah could see in the faces of many that her mission to give people hugs might not be as difficult as she thought earlier. Hannah, as her mother, could feel the hope in the air as Jesus spoke.

Jesus may leave tomorrow, but they both had a feeling that the village would never be the same.

2

The Adoption

After Jesus left, life in the village went back to it's normal routine. But the atmosphere around the village was much different. Many of the villagers came to believe that Jesus truly was the Messiah because of the message he brought them. A message of love as they had never heard before. There was a lot of talk around the village about this new way of looking at God. Those who believed what Jesus spoke of knew that they needed to transition from their mechanical ways of doing things and start looking for ways to do things on a more emotional level.

This was the challenge for everyone, as there was no examples anywhere that reflected a life lived emotionally. Nobody ever talked about emotions. Most marriages were business transactions by a father and a man and had nothing to do with the emotions of love. If you were Jewish, Samaritan, Roman or anything else, you did not see anywhere people who lived life on an emotional level. It's just not the way people lived their lives at the time, so the message of love that Jesus spoke of sounded great, but did not come with any understanding of how you were to change your ways and start living an emotional life.

So the debates around the village were certainly energetic as the townspeople tried to figure out what traditions and rules needed to stay and what needed to go. You couldn't possibly just abandon everything you have been brought up to believe and just start loving one another, right?

The Samaritans in the village, as well as the many who heard the message Jesus was speaking, understood the message. God is love. God wants us to live a spiritual life with emotions. God wants everything we do to come from a foundation built on love. Love of God, love of neighbor, love of thyself. That all sounded great, but how exactly do we apply that to our traditions and lifestyles that have been passed on to us from generation to generation? It created a lot of confusion as the debates became more layered with questions than answers.

This quiet Samaritan village was growing frustrated at all the debates with everyone having an opinion but nobody having any real answers.

It was in this environment of chaos and debate that Hannah quietly and persistently provided the answer.

She started every morning by giving her mother a big hug and telling her how much she loved her. It had a impact on Ruth as she learned to appreciate her role as Hannah's mother every day. She was in a good mood most days and didn't seem to mind all the chores and work needed to survive her simple life. She had turned away her male friend by telling him he was not welcome to come by any more unless he was willing to commit to a life of honest love for her and her daughter, which got him quickly heading down the road, never looking back again. Ruth learned to forgive herself for her past choices and no longer looked at herself as an outcast in society. People will believe what they want to believe and she believed the God that Jesus spoke of was truly a God of love and forgiveness. If others continued to shut her out, that was their choice. She was just going to continue to love Hannah and be kind to others regardless.

Every day, Hannah would walk around the village and greet the people with an offer for a hug. Of course, she mostly got turned away, but Hannah was always quick to replay, "Okay, I hope you have a nice day." She felt a little sad as everyone seemed to talk a lot about Jesus, but for the most part, nobody was really doing anything but arguing.

"I don't understand why nobody wants a hug." Hannah said to her mother one night.

"Oh Hannah, I wouldn't worry about it too much. Most people would rather debate and argue about something instead of actually doing something. Love is a new idea to many people and for most, it's not easy to give up your traditions and go in a new direction. But at least you know that I will never turn down a hug from you." says Ruth as she embraces Hannah.

"It's frustrating because I know that if they just give it a try, they are going to see how easy it is to love people." Hannah says.

"You're right, Hannah, but they will come around. You just have to never give up and one of these days, someone is going to hug you and realize how special you are and before long, everyone else is going to want Hannah's hugs."

Ruth was right of course. It wasn't long before one of the villagers gave Hannah a hug. He was an older man named Saul who owned a number of goats just outside of the village, who came to the village square every now and then to sell his goat milk and cheese to anyone who needed them.

Saul was a good man who had a very loving heart and truly loved his life and the people in it. He often let Hannah help him sell his products and visit with the goat he would always bring with him, so it wasn't a surprise to see that he would be the first to let Hannah give him a hug.

One day, as Hannah went into town to visit Saul, he was not there. This was not unusual, as Saul would only come into town when he had a good supply of goat products to sell. But after four days, Hannah became concerned and asked her mother if she could go out to Saul's place to see if he was okay. Ruth didn't want Hannah going out there alone and agreed to go with her.

Saul's place was a good mile or more northeast of the village, while Ruth and Hannah lived on the outskirts southwest of the village nearest to Jacobs well, so this was going to be a pretty good hike for the two, but they didn't mind. They left early enough before the hot mid-day heat could affect them and it was a beautiful morning for a walk.

When they got to their destination, they could see the goats grazing on the hillside just behind Sauls home. They called out for Saul and heard his voice in response coming from inside his home, so Ruth and Hannah went in.

They found Saul sitting near his fire pit with one leg propped up and covered with blankets and rags as Hannah rushed to give him a hug.

"I missed you coming to the village, so we came out here to see if you were okay." said Hannah with a warm, embracing hug.

"How kind of you, Hannah. I took a spill the other day up on the hill and hurt my leg. I'm unable to get around much, let alone go all the way into the village." said Saul.

Hannah stepped back from Saul with a sad face, "I'm sorry you're feeling bad. Is there anything we can do to help?"

Saul smiles at the generous little girl. "There's not much to do but wait for the leg to heal."

Hannah looks at Saul's leg, which is covered by rags, then to her mother before she turns to Saul again.

"Maybe we could stay here for awhile and help with the goats until you're leg gets better." she says.

Saul smiles at Hannah and looks to Ruth who follows up.

"We could help with the goats and give you the time to rest and get your leg healed." she smiles, "If you don't mind the company, of course."

Hannah doesn't give Saul a chance to speak as her excitement is out of control.

"Can you show me how to make the cheese and how to take care of the goats?" she says with so much enthusiasm, it makes it pretty hard for Saul to resist the invitation.

"If you don't mind a broken down old man hobbling around telling you what to do." he says with a smile as Hannah gives him a big hug.

For the remainder of the day, Hannah and Ruth settle into a routine of helping Saul. Ruth got some water from a nearby well and cleaned Sauls wounded leg as Hannah listened intensely to Saul's instructions for working with the goats.

While Hannah was outside gathering all his goats to bring them into the shaded manger, she found a strong branch that she thought would make a fine walking stick for Saul as his leg got batter.

By nightfall, Saul, Hannah and Ruth had everything in order and were able to enjoy a quiet evening of relaxing by the fire. Saul was especially happy as he seldom had company and was more than happy to have Ruth and Hannah staying with him.

While Hannah and Ruth worked on the branch that would become a cane for Saul, they talked a lot about all the chores to take care of his goats. You could tell that Saul loved his goats and seemed to have more concern for their well being than he was his leg. It was clear that he was very grateful to have Ruth and Hannah around to help with his beloved goats.

After a few days, Ruth and Hannah had become very helpful to Saul, Hannah learning so much about taking care of his goats and how to make the cheese, while Ruth worked to take care of Saul.

Hannah and Ruth even started to make a few trips into the village to sell Saul's goat cheese and milk. While there, Hannah always offered hugs to those who wanted to purchase her products and was always telling the people to have a nice day. While Hannah was busy selling product and telling villagers about Saul's health, Ruth would go to her home to collect some personal items for her and Hannah to have while they were at Sauls.

One evening, after Hannah had fallen asleep, Saul turned to Ruth with an idea.

"You and Hannah have been such a big help for me and I know that I am old with very little time left in this world. I have no family and would like to make you and Hannah my family, so I know my goats will be taken care of after I leave."

Ruth is touched by Saul's words. She has never heard anyone talk to her like that.

"You are very kind to say such words, Saul, but your leg will get better."

Ruth was becoming a bit concerned, however, as Saul's leg really wasn't healing as quickly as she had hoped. Saul's age probably was contributing to his inability to get around much, but she also feared that there was more than just the injury to his leg as Saul's breathing and energy were very troubling as he seemed to suffer a great deal of pain whenever he tried to move around. She suspected that his fall on the hill was a lot more than a simple cut on his leg.

"Ruth I know it is more than my leg that is broken. My body tells me my time is not much more. When you and Hannah go into the village tomorrow, I want you to ask Joseph, one of the village leaders, to come back with you so I can talk to him. I want him to know that I have adopted you and Hannah so that when my time comes, I know my goats will be taken care of."

Ruth's eyes begin to water as she looks at this broken, kind man with such a generous heart. She doesn't know how to respond to such a proposal.

"You are too kind, Saul, but we must work on getting you better." she says.

Saul leans up to Ruth and looks deeply into her eyes, "Promise me you will bring Joseph to me tomorrow. He loves my cheese and I know he will listen to me if he wants to continue to get his cheese." He says with a big smile.

When Hannah and Ruth go into the village the next day, Ruth sees Joseph talking with some of the other village leaders. She is hesitant to approach, especially in front of the others, because they have always treated her and Hannah as very marginal people and didn't think he would agree to go back to Sauls with her.

Fortunately, Ruth didn't have to approach Joseph. When he saw her and Hannah setting up their table with cheese, he made his way over to them.

"Where is Saul? Why are you selling his goods?" Joseph says with an unfriendly tone.

Hannah is quick to respond in her bright and cheerful way, "He had a fall, so mother and I are helping him out with his goats. Would you like some cheese?"

Joseph hesitates in thought, "Yes girl, that would be fine." he pulls out some coins but hesitates to hand it over to these two.

"How do I know Saul will get this money?" he asks.

Ruth responds with a strong dose of assurance, "Joseph, my daughter and I have been helping Saul out for some time and I assure you we have asked for nothing in return. He is not well and has asked me to have you go to his home and speak with him."

Joseph looks at Ruth with uncertainty. "I will go to him alone and speak with him." he says clearly insinuating he will not go with them, then he looks at Hannah. "And I will take the money for the cheese to Saul personally." he says as he puts the coins back in his possession.

"Okay. Have a nice day," says Hannah in her cheerful manner.

As Joseph heads out towards Sauls home, Ruth and Hannah remain to sell his products until it is all gone, then head back to Sauls.

As they approach Sauls home, Hannah is quick to run ahead to show Saul how much money he has made from his cheese. She stops at the entry when she sees Joseph, but Saul is quick to invite her in.

"Hannah, come in. How did it go in the village?"

Hannah runs over to Saul and hands him a bag with some coins.

"You did well. People really like your cheese Mr. Saul." as she gives him a hug and Ruth enters the home behind her.

"I couldn't have done it without you, little girl." Saul says.

He looks at Joseph and then back at Hannah.

"I was just telling Joseph how much help you and your mother have been for me and that I would like to adopt you both as my family. Would that be okay with you Hannah?"

Hannah looks over to her mother and then to Saul, not quite sure what he means.

"What does adopt mean?" she asks.

"It means you and your mother can live here like family and help me take care of the goats." Saul says.

Hannah again looks to her mother with excitement. "Is that okay with you mother?"

Ruth hesitates and looks to Joseph who is looking at her with unenthusiastic resolve, then back to Hannah.

"This is very kind of Saul to do, Hannah. Being adopted by Saul, we must honor him as a father and do whatever we can be please him, okay Hannah?"

Hannah is excited. "Does it mean I can stay and help with the goats and make more cheese?" she says to Saul.

"Yes Hannah, you will be responsible of taking care of my goats and making sure the people in the village have the best cheese they've ever had."

Hannah gives Saul another big hug as he looks at her.

"Now it's getting late so why don't you go get them and bring them in for the evening."

"Okay." says Hannah with great enthusiasm as she turns and runs out the front door.

Saul looks over to Joseph, who has been taking this all in quietly.

"So Joseph, as you have witnessed, you will agree to let anyone who questions know that Ruth and Hannah are my family and the village will continue to have my cheese and milk as long as my family is here?"

Joseph concedes and looks to Ruth.

"You understand that if Saul adopts you and Hannah, you must obey his wishes and submit to him in every way?" he asks her.

Ruth looks to Saul, then back to Joseph.

"We will submit to Saul as his family and do whatever he wishes."

With that, Joseph stands and prepares to leave.

"Let it be as you have spoken today, Saul. From this day, Ruth and Hannah will be your family as you have wished. I must leave before dark." he says as he heads out the entrance without any further comment.

As he heads down the road, he looks over to see Hannah guiding the goats to their manger. She smiles and waves at Joseph.

"Have a nice day, Mr. Joseph."

Joseph simply smiles as he watches her for a minute before turning and heading back to the village.

3

Saul's Goodbye

Life for Saul, Ruth and Hannah settles into a family routine. Saul's health improved enough for him to be able to get around with the cane Hannah and Ruth made him, but his age had certainly slowed him down. Having Ruth and Hannah around not only made his life easier, but his spirits seemed to be much more upbeat and happy. Saul truly enjoyed the company and had no doubt that if Hannah and Ruth had not come out to check on him those many months ago, he would have surely died and his goats would have been left on their own.

For Ruth, life was better now than ever before. Saul had become a very loving father figure to her. Having grown up never knowing who her father was and a mother dying when she was young teenager, she really embraced the new family setting with Saul and Hannah. She was happy to do the chores and help both Hannah and Saul maintain a comfortable life in their simple home.

For Hannah, life simply couldn't get any better. She loved working with the goats and had become quite good at producing the cheese and milk that people came to expect in the village. Her and her mother would head to the village every other day or so to sell more cheese and milk, as Hannah had become a positive fixture in the village. Her cheerful, have a nice day disposition was addictive and she was finding more and more people – mostly the women – happy to grab a hug from Hannah, who was always offering with every sale.

Ruth had a small garden of herbs and spices in the back that she delighted in maintaining that her and Hannah could add to their cheese and give the villagers different options of flavors. Their reputation grew as word got out that if you were traveling, you needed to stop by the village and get some cheese, spices and herbs from Hannah.

Life was good. Joseph would come by from time to time to check on his old friend. His visits were not so innocent as simply visiting an old friend though. He clearly didn't trust Ruth and Hannah and believed there were sinister motives to the adoption. He was convinced that Ruth was planning on killing Saul so her and Hannah could have complete control of his home. Yet every time Joseph came to visit Saul, he found nothing but positive activity.

Ruth would be out in her garden or in the manger working on their products with little conversation with Joseph outside of answering any questions he had. Hannah was busy playing and working with her goats in her normal positive manner. Saul was always in his home or sitting outside observing his family and appreciating how much these women have added to his life.

Every conversation with Saul was glowing with how much Hannah and Ruth have made his life so much better. Of course, it didn't help Joseph that Hannah would always stop what she was doing when she saw him walking up the road and run to give him a hug that was not encouraged and a warm greeting.

This little girl, who was quickly moving into her adolescent years, was so positive and compassionate about her work, that it made Joseph keenly aware that any case he had against Ruth and Hannah would be very hard to sell to the villagers who had become so enthralled with Hannah every time her and her mother came to sell their products. She was quickly becoming the girl with the wonderful cheese and warm hugs around the village and most looked forward to those days when Hannah and Ruth would show up to sell their products.

It remained this way for quite a long time. The only thing that changed was that everyone was getting older. Saul became fragile in his advanced age and spent most of his time sitting inside his home or outside watching Hannah tend to his goats.

Ruth had become much older than her mid-forties would suggest. She worked so hard and had such a rough road in her life, that she was ageing a lot quicker than the calendar. Still, maintaining her garden and working with Hannah to produce their products for the villagers gave her great comfort and joy, regardless of the aches and pains she took to bed with her every night.

For Hannah, she had become a young lady in her early twenties. Though her body matured, her positive disposition had remained unchanged. She was always a welcome sight to the villagers whenever she came to sell her products. She didn't have to ask people for hugs any more as they were always the start of any conversation.

She was coming into the village on her own for the most part, as Ruth understood that her daughter was old enough to handle things on her own. Besides, Ruth enjoyed the break and could often be found sitting with Saul enjoying a conversation when Hannah returned from her trips into the village.

One day, Hannah was preparing for another trip into the village when she asked her mother if she wanted to go with her. This wasn't unusual, as Hannah often invited her mother to come along and it wasn't unusual for Ruth to say yes and joining her daughter for the trip into the village. Ruth was feeling good and thought a nice walk into the village with her daughter would be great.

After checking with Saul to make sure that he had everything he needed and would be okay on his own, the two gave Saul a hug and a kiss on his cheek and set out for a day in the village.

It was a great day in the village. Everyone seemed pleasant and in good spirits. Being early Fall, it was easy to be in good spirits as the hot, dry days of Summer were behind them, quickly giving way to the much milder days of the season, so people wanted to be outside. Hannah always made the day better with her positive disposition and eagerness to give out hugs to all that came by.

This is why Ruth was willing to come with her now and then. She would reflect on how difficult her and Hannah had it when they lived out by Jacobs well, so she truly appreciated how much the people enjoyed her daughter, and how many were even willing to give her a hug as well. Though she understood that the hugs she received were much more guarded and more obligatory, it was still a long ways from the days when she would have to go to the well in midday by herself to get her water.

Ruth often thought about Jesus and her encounter with him those many years ago. She thought a lot about his message of love and especially gave a lot of thought to the idea of an unconditional love. It was his message of love that made Ruth strong, as she understood that if it wasn't for Hannah, these same villagers would have nothing to do with her. But she also knew that it was Hannah who set the example for all that Jesus had taught them.

Ruth suspected that many of the villagers were coming to understand that. Love was not something to debate. Love was not something that needed a set of rules to follow. Love was a feeling of simply caring about one another and the world they lived in. Ruth was seeing that it was Hannah's hugs and positive approach to living that spoke more about the message Jesus gave them than all the debating in the world. One by one, these Samaritans were coming around to understanding that the persistence of Hannah's love was exactly the message of love that Jesus had brought them.

Ruth thought a lot about Jesus. She had heard that he was killed a few years back and some said he rose again from the dead. She wasn't sure how much of this was true or not, but it never really mattered to her. She knew from the conversation she had with him that he was the Messiah and whatever happened to him after he left their village would not change her thinking.

It was a good day at the village and as Hannah and Ruth sold the last of their products, they packed up and started to make their way back to their home. It was a great day with a nice breeze, so Hannah and Ruth seemed to be in no hurry.

As they reached their home, they went in and found Joseph sitting by a very lifeless Saul in his chair.

Ruth dropped everything and ran to Saul and could tell right away that Saul had passed away. She turned to Joseph, "What happened to Saul?" she asked as Hannah ran to her mother with tears.

"Maybe you could tell me." said Joseph very accusingly.

Ruth knew that Joseph didn't trust her and knew exactly where he wanted to take this conversation.

"Hannah and I have been in the village all day."

"How convenient he should die on the same day you both went into the village."

Ruth takes a deep breath as her old self is screaming inside at this man's accusations that she would have anything to do with Saul's passing. She thinks of Jesus' message of love, before replying to Joseph.

"Saul was like a father to us. We loved this man very much. If you will leave us now, Hannah and I have to prepare him for burial."

Joseph stands and sternly says, "You will leave his body as is and I will have someone come to prepare his body. We will decide later what to do with you and Hannah." He looks at Hannah, who is crying, "And I will take today's profits with me. We will also decide what, if any, profits you two should receive from Saul's estate."

He reaches out his hand as Hannah looks to her mother.

"Give the man the money, Hannah. It's not worth it." says Ruth as she looks at Joseph with cold eyes.

"I will be back with a couple of other men to take care of Saul. Until the village leaders decide your fate, you are welcome to stay here for now."

With that, Joseph leaves as Hannah crumbles into Ruth's lap weeping.

~~~~~~~~~~

As the two men with Joseph made a burial site for Saul behind the home, Joseph tells Ruth and Hannah that the village leaders will meet in the morning to discuss their fates and they best be there. Ruth agrees without a word as Joseph and the grave diggers head down the road.

"Why is Joseph doing this to us mother?" asks Hannah, "We would never do anything to harm Saul and he knows it." she says frustrated.
~~~~~~~~~~

"Joseph is an angry, sad man, Hannah. We have a past that makes him treat me as if I am a dog. He lives on lies because the truth is too much for him to face. I am certain that he will do all he can to make my life – and unfortunately yours, too- miserable."

"But it's just not right," Hannah says, "We have done nothing but love Saul with all our hearts and now because of Joseph we may lose everything?"

Ruth smiles at Hannah, "We may well lose our home and our goats, but we will never lose the truth. We must trust God and stay true to the truth and let the villagers decide what they will."

"Well it doesn't seem like we have much of a chance." Hannah says bowing her head in a defeatists posture.

Ruth lifts Hannah's head and smiles, "We must trust God no matter and stand firmly on the truth," she hesitates and smiles broadly at Hannah, "Besides, if they take away our goats, they will have no more cheese."

Hannah gives her mother a big hug.

4

———

The Trial

"We are here to discuss the death of our friend Saul. We will first hear from the accuser." says the village leader, Simon, as everyone settles into their places.

Ruth and Hannah are seated next to the village leader as Joseph stands to speak.

"It is well known that this woman has a past. She has lived an unsavory lifestyle as we all know. It has been my observation that Ruth tricked Saul into this alleged adoption with a motive of getting rid of Saul so her and her daughter could profit from his estate. It is not surprising to me at all that Saul would pass away on the very day that both Ruth and Hannah were here in the village selling Saul's product. We all know how hard Ruth worked on her garden and it is more than suspicious that the herbs and other plants she grew could easily have created a special 'potion', if you will, that would have created the perfect alibi as they came to the village."

"Do you have any evidence or proof to offer?" asked the village leader.

"I do not. But when I went out to check on Saul, it was obvious that this woman went out of her way to create the appearance of a natural death. All the food and drink neatly set up next to Saul to give one the impression that nothing sinister is at work. It clearly appeared to me that this woman was playing us for fools."

The village leader stands as Joseph sits, "We have heard from the accuser. We shall now hear a response from the accused."

Ruth stands and looks out at the villagers, looks at Joseph, who refuses to even look at her, before she begins.

"I am well aware of my past. I am well aware that there are people here who will never let my past go away. But Jesus knew my past as well. I will always be grateful that I spoke with this Jewish man at the well that day. I will always be grateful that this man came and stayed with us all for those few days. I will always be grateful for the message he gave all of us. He spoke of love – a love unlike anything we have heard before. He treated my young daughter with a kindness unlike anything we have seen before. It was Hannah's love for people and animals that connected with Saul. It was Hannah who grew concerned when Saul had not come into the village for a few days and insisted that we go to his home to check on him. It was Hannah who insisted that we stay with Saul and help him with his goats while he recovered from his injuries from a fall."

Ruth pauses and gathers strength before she continues.

"It was Saul who wanted to adopt Hannah and I. He knew his injuries and age would slow him down and he wanted to continue to produce the products that so many of you enjoyed. When the adoption was made public, as witnessed by the accuser himself, Hannah and I became Saul's family. We worked hard to provide the best possible products we could to honor Saul for his kindness. At no time did Hannah or myself ever take any money from Saul. We loved the life that Saul had given to us and being family was always enough."

Ruth again pauses before continuing.

"We have done nothing wrong. By our hard work, Hannah and I have made the last years of Saul's life one of comfort. We will miss Saul, and we hope to honor his life by continuing to work with his goats and provide this village with our products. We ask nothing more."

Ruth sits down as the villagers look at one another, some whispering, some just speechless, before the village leader stands again.

"We have heard from the accuser and the accused. I will now ask them to leave and return to their homes while the rest of us discuss the matter." He turns to Hannah and Ruth and says, "You may go back to the home for now until we come out with the villagers decision."

As Ruth and Hannah leave, Joseph gets up and is quick to get the last word as he is leaving, "Don't keep falling for her lies."

As Hannah and Ruth make their way back to their home, they are quiet for the most part with only a spattering of comments of how anyone could think that they were responsible for Saul's passing. Hannah was especially troubled by the chain of events lately. She was a young woman now who had become so much involved with the herd of goats and providing the best cheese to everyone at the village. She just couldn't imagine what she would do if they decided to take all that away from her now. She grew up understanding how her and her mother were outsiders and not well thought of by the villagers. She knew her mother had made bad choices in her youth, but she also knew that she had changed her ways.

But mostly, she knew how much her and her mother cared about Saul and had nothing by loving memories of this man who adopted them and made their life so worthwhile. Now because one man has made an accusation that has no merit of any kind, Hannah feared that they would be left homeless and rejected by the community they loved to served.

Hannah didn't feel much like hugging anyone right now.

After a quiet day with Hannah out with the goats and Ruth working her garden, the village leader, Joseph and two other villagers came up the road. As everyone gathered at the home, the village leaders did not hesitate to get right to the point.

"After discussing the matter and having only the accuser's word against the accused's word, the village leaders have determined a compromise." he pauses as both Ruth and Hannah take a deep breath as Joseph stands tall with confidence. "Ruth, you and Hannah may remain in this home and continue working the goats as before. However, every time you sell your products in the village, you must give all proceeds to me, as the village leader, and I will decide any compensation you might warrant to continue your work. All other profits will remain in the village treasury, to be used as needed to the benefit of the village." Again he pauses before continuing, "I have brought witnesses and proclaimed this decision before both the accuser and the accused so that there may not be any further discussion. Do both parties agree to the terms of this decision?"

He looks to Joseph, who hesitates, looks to Ruth with disgust, then to the village leader, "If this is the will of the village, but I will never dignify their decision by buying any of these liars products." he says in a very cold tone.

Simon responds, "The village will have no say in who buys or does not buy products from these women." He turns to Ruth and Hannah for their response as Ruth speaks,

"We will continue to work hard to bring the best products possible to the village with the proceeds going to you."

The village leader turns to the two witnesses that were there, "We have understood the terms of this verdict and will consider the matter closed from this day forward."

The witnesses nod in agreement and the village leaders turns back to Ruth and Hannah, "We will leave you now to your work. Good afternoon." he says as they all turn to leave.

Joseph looks to Ruth, "Once again you got what you wanted."

Ruth cooly replies, "And once again, you did not."

Joseph turns in disgust and quickly heads down the road, not talking to any of the others.

5

___

The Visiters

As Ruth and Hannah settled into a routine in their home, life became somewhat normal for the two women. Ruth was getting older and slowing down more now, and seldom went with Hannah into the village. She felt good about how life turned out for her and Hannah and they would often spend their evenings, after all the chores were done, sitting in their home talking about the love they had learned from Jesus and what they might do to become more loving people.

They had built a reputation with their goat products through the years as it was not unusual for travelers from the north or south to stop by their home to pick up some products on their way. Hannah always made sure to give the village leader any money she received from the travelers as they had agreed to do.

The trial had changed Hannah somewhat. She was still the positive, warm woman, but had become a bit guarded when she was in the village. She believed what her mother had told her, that the villagers didn't condemn them only because they wanted their products, which made her sad. She thought it was unfair that they had to give all their proceeds to the village leader and they had to practically beg to get any of the money to improve their lives at home.

Hannah was still generous with her hugs, but for the most part, the hugs were for the village children. As the village grew, there were more children about the village and Hannah was always happy to give out hugs and treats to the children. She also loved talking to any child that would listen about the man she met when she was a little girl. She was always encouraging the children to give people – especially their parents – hugs and tell them to have a nice day.

As promised, Joseph refused to buy any product from Hannah and never spoke to her. She tried to be pleasant to him, but his refusal to acknowledge her in any way pretty much let her know he would never let go of whatever it was that made him dislike her and her mother so much. Hannah was gaining more warmth from the village leader as she truly remained honest and consistent in turning over all the proceeds from her products. He was becoming more convinced that the village had misjudged Hannah and her mother and had become much more generous in letting Hannah keep some of the proceeds to help her out at home.

One day, when Hannah left early with her products to sell at the village, Ruth stayed behind as normal. She had not been feeling well and looked forward to a quiet day of rest. As she settled into her quiet morning, she heard some voices outside.

It didn't frighten her as travelers often went by her home on their way north or south, and they sounded happy with a conversation mixed with laughter.

"I think this is the place. There are some goats on the hill behind it." said one voice. "Hello. Is anybody here?" yells the voice.

Ruth gets up and moves to the front door and opens it to find four men who have obviously been traveling a great distance.

"Sorry to bother you, but we are traveling into Jerusalem and I was hoping to find a woman named Hannah." the older man says.

That got Ruth's attention for sure, but she was still a bit hesitant, though respectful. "That is my daughter." she says.

The older man raises his hands in victory and smiles, "Ah, then you must be Ruth! It is a delight to be in your presence." he says as he makes his way up to Ruth, who is a bit confused. "My name is Paul. I am a disciple of Jesus and these are my companions. We have heard many great things about the Samaritan women that Jesus spoke with from many of my brothers who followed him. We would be honored to take a rest with you, if we may?"

"You knew Jesus?" asks Ruth as she relaxes with the friendly greeting.

"Unfortunately, I did not. I converted to his teachings shortly after he was crucified. But I love talking to people who did know him and would love to hear your story." he says as they stop in front of her.

Ruth opens the door fully, "Of course, you are welcome." she says

As they make their way in, Ruth realizes she has little to offer them as Hannah took all the product into the village.

"I am sorry, Hannah is in the village selling our products. I'm afraid I have very little to offer you to eat or drink." she says.

Paul laughs, "From what I hear, it is unlikely that young Hannah will be bringing any of her product back with her. Best goat cheese in the region from what I hear. We have provisions that we would gladly share with you. These are my companions, Marcus, Luke and Barnabas."

As they all greet Ruth and sit down, Paul is not one to wait for a conversation to start, so he begins. "I have talked to many who traveled with Jesus and they spoke so highly of the time Jesus spoke with you and spent a few days with you and Hannah. They say that Jesus always talked to his followers about Gods love being for everyone and used the Samaritan woman at the well as an example. He often told those who would listen to be like children and often used Hannah as an example. It is an honor to be in the presence of someone Jesus spoke so highly of."

Ruth is humbled by this man's words, "Jesus was a kind and generous man. He spoke of love like no other person had before. I have carried his teachings of Gods love in my heart through the years, and Hannah as well. It is that love and Gods mercy that has provided for us through the years."

Paul is hanging on every word. He clearly loves talking to

someone who actually knew Jesus and he knows this woman is going to enlighten him so much more about the man he preaches about in his travels.

"Tell me how he spoke of love." he asks Ruth.

"He spoke of love like no one I have every heard before. Love if patient and kind. Love never fails. Love protects, trusts and hopes. It never boasts or envies or is proud. You could see in his eyes the compassion in his soul. Though I had never met this man before, he knew my past and encouraged me to let go of my past as God's love is forgiving and unconditional. He treated Hannah and I with so much kindness. His visit changed our life forever and I am truly grateful to God that I was at that well on that day."

Paul is enthralled by every word Ruth speaks. As they settle into an afternoon of sharing stories and provisions, there is much laughter and love. Ruth is enjoying these visitors so much and is feeling much more energized by their stay. She is in no hurry to get them back on the road and insists that they stay until Hannah returns so she can meet them.

As the late afternoon sun starts to sink behind the hills, Ruth can hear the bell of the goat and knows Hannah is home. After she puts everything away in the manger, Hannah comes into the home to find her mother surrounded by these four visitors, and stops.

"Hannah, come in and meet these men who are followers of Jesus." says Ruth with much enthusiasm as Paul, Luke, Marcus and Barnabas stand up to greet her.

"So this is Hannah, the little girl that Jesus taught to hug people. You have become quite a young woman now, but do you still give out hugs?" says Paul with a warm smile and open arms.

Hannah hesitates and looks at her mother who encourages her to respond, so Hannah smiles at Paul and gives him a hug. Then she follows with a hug for the other three as they all settle down again.

"Hannah, these men have been traveling all over the world telling people the message of love that Jesus taught us. They have been here all day waiting because they wanted to meet you." says Ruth.

Hannah smiles, "I need to go get the goats back into the manger. I am sorry I have sold out all of our cheese and will not have more for another day." she says.

"Well I hear that it's the best cheese in the region, so I'm not surprised, Hannah. But we came to see you and your mother, so we have our own provisions we can share with you." Paul gets up and continues, "Let me go with you and help get those wild beasts back into their home." he says without waiting for an answer as he walks out the door as Hannah looks to her mother, smiles and turns to follow him out.

As Barnabas, Marcus and Luke stay behind to visit with Ruth, Hannah and Paul head up the hillside to gather the goats in for the evening.

"I am so glad we were able to meet you Hannah. And your mother, too. I wasn't sure if she was still alive, since it had been many years." said Paul.

"Well she's been slowing down for sure, but your visit has really rekindled her spirits. She's had a rough life, you know."

"Yes I know, but it is good that she has made peace with herself. Your mother has a good heart, I can tell."

"I'm not sure how much longer she has, but I always pray that God gives her peace, either here or when he takes her home."

"Oh Hannah, I know God will create a heaven for both you and your mother that reflects the love you gave to so many here in this life."

Paul claps his hands to redirect the goats and head them towards the manger before he continues, "How are the villagers treating you and your mother. I understand that your mother was not favored by many in the village?"

"That's an understatement. She has admitted that she made some bad choices in her youth, but they are not nearly as bad as what the rumors and talk around the village suggest. The man who made mother pregnant with me abandoned us and has never been heard from again. Some believe that mother killed him, others say she had relations with so many men they would never know who my true father was. It's a reputation that is hard to break no matter how truthful you are."

"What do you know to be the truth, Hannah?"

"I know that my mother would have married my father, but he left as soon as he found out she was pregnant. She was heartbroken and left to go through the whole pregnancy alone. No one in the village came to help her. Even when I was born, there was no one to help my mother."

"Is that why they accused you of killing Saul?"

Hannah looks at Paul with a surprised look before he responds, "She told us earlier about the trial. One of the village leaders, Joseph I believe is his name, brought the case against you and your mother."

"Mother says that Joseph has history with her that she does not talk about, but it clearly seems as if Joseph does all he can to make our lives miserable."

"Do you think he might be your father?" Paul asks.

"No. My mother is clear on that. Something went on between her and Joseph, but it was never that kind of relationship. She doesn't want to talk about it, but I suspect maybe he knew my father and he probably thinks mother killed him, too. Whatever it is, he sure goes out of his way to make life miserable for us."

Paul smiles at Hannah, "Maybe I could visit with him when we pass through the village."

"Joseph is a leader in the village that has great influence. You may not want to start anything with that man. He is what he is." says Hannah.

Paul smiles, "Well Hannah, my experience says that God's love is built on the foundation of truth and has a lot more influence than any man who lives on a foundation of lies."

Hannah smiles, "Just be careful. Some hearts are just made of stone."

"A heart made of stone can turn to lava in God's presence."

Paul and his companions decide to spend the night with Ruth and Hannah before they head south in the cool of the morning.

The next morning, Hannah says her goodbyes to the travelers as she heads out to the manger to milk her goats and get them out to the hills while it's still cool. Paul tells the other three to start without him as he wants to have a final word with Ruth, who had a rough night sleeping and is still reclined inside.

"Before I leave you, Ruth, I want you to tell me the truth of something that bothers me."

"I have told you the truth in everything, Paul." she responds.

"Yes you have Ruth. But I want to know what happened to make Joseph so hateful towards you and Hannah. Did you have a relations with him?"

Ruth speaks with a strong voice, "No! … and that IS the issue!"

Paul hesitates in thought of what she just said, before Ruth clarifies.

"That's what everyone believes. The truth is that Joseph made several advances towards me but I refused him every time. I knew his wife – we were friends growing up – and I would never let a married man take advantage of me. He got frustrated knowing I was not going to give in. Then he tried to pay me to be quiet about his advances, but I refused his money. Ever since then he's gone out of his way to make stories up about me to the villagers so if I ever said anything about him, he could easily call me a liar."

Ruth takes a deep breath as Paul looks at her, realizing this is likely the first time she has said anything about this, before she adds, "I have done nothing to offend this man. I respected his wife too much to have stooped to the level of being a mistress for his convenience."

Ruth's face is strong with conviction and purpose, as Paul embraces her with a hug like no other hug.

Tears streaming from his eyes, Paul looks at Ruth, "I am so sorry for the injustices you have carried because of this man. There is much I do not understand, but I now fully understand why Jesus spoke so highly of the Samaritan woman at the well. You are a woman of great strength, courage and Love. Soon, God will take you home to reap your inheritance that you so richly deserve. I will think of you and Hannah often Ruth, and I promise to share your message of love … and Hannah's hugs… to all I speak to."

With another warm embrace, Paul gets up and leaves to join his companions, as Ruth lays down and weeps in exhaustion.

6

Farewell

After the visitors, life settled back down to a normal routine for both Hannah and Ruth, though Ruth's health prevented her from being much help to her daughter. But on those 'good' days, Ruth was always willing to get out and at least give Hannah instructions for creating a great garden.

As expected, Hannah took to her garden chores as she did the goats. She loved her work and always wanted to learn as much as she could so she could always improve her products. Hannah had established a pretty consistent routine. She would take her products into the village every third day. This gave her two days to work the goats and garden and create the products, then the third day would be spent in the village selling her products.

Hannah always enjoyed heading into the village. She was always pleasant to the villagers, even though most of them treated her on a very business like level without engaging much in conversations with her. Only a handful of the villagers actually spoke to her, but Hannah never complained. She could always rely on the children coming by for treats and stories.

She loved her life and loved providing the best products for her neighbors. As long as she could continue to live the simple life that she had, she was not going to worry much about what the villagers thought about her and her mother. She knew they loved her products, which she almost always sold out of by mid-day, and that was enough for Hannah.

On this particular trip into the village, Hannah noticed a change in the atmosphere. People seemed more pleasant to Hannah as many complimented her and asked about her mother. This was unusual, but Hannah was encouraged.

As she sold the last of her product, Hannah prepared to head back home. Of course, her first stop would be to the village leader, Simon, to turn over her profits from the day. As she was handing her money over to Simon, he cupped his hands around hers and looked at Hannah with gentle eyes.

"From now on Hannah, you and your mother may keep everything."

Hannah looks at Simon in a confused manner before he removes his hands from hers and continues.

"Hannah, do you recall a visitor you had named Paul?"

Hannah smiles curiously, "Yes. He was a follower of Jesus."

"Yes he was. After he left your home, he went into Jerusalem to take care of some business, but when he left, he made it a point to come back here to talk with me." He pauses as Hannah looks at Simon even more curious. "He told me everything your mother told him and opened my eyes to the truth about your mother. Hannah, we have judged your mother harshly based on false rumors and hearsay. I wish to come with you back to your home and ask your mother for forgiveness on behalf of the entire village."

Hannah looks at Simon with tears of gratitude welling up in her eyes, even though she was unaware of the conversation Paul had with her mother before he left. As Hannah agrees to have Simon go with her to her home, Simon lets others know that he will be back in the morning, as it was late afternoon and would not be safe to walk back to the village after dark.

As they made their way towards Hannah's home, she wanted to know more.

"I was unaware that my mother spoke with Paul at any length. What did he tell you?"

"He said that on the morning he left, he asked Ruth to tell him the truth about Joseph and what made him so hateful towards her. At first, she didn't want to say anything, but Paul was very persuasive in encouraging her to speak the truth. She recalled that when she was much younger, Joseph tried on many occasions to have his way with her, but she refused his advances. His wife, Martha and her were good friends growing up and she would never dishonor the friendship by letting Joseph have his way with her. When Joseph realized he would not get his way, he offered Ruth money in order to keep her from telling Martha or anyone else. But your mother refused his money as well. Ever since then, Joseph has spread rumors about your mother that had no basis other than to give him credibility if she ever accused him of his attempts to be an adulterer. Even after Martha died, Joseph continued to do all he could to prevent your mother from exposing him."

Hannah stops as tears flow out of her eyes and prevents her from continuing. She looks at Simon and he sees the shock in her face.

"Were you unaware of this? Did your mother not even tell you?"

Hannah shakes her head no, "She only said that her and Joseph had a past, but would never elaborate."

Simon pauses as he realized how Ruth kept her secret to herself through all the years of being shunned by the villagers.

"Your mother kept that in her heart all these years. Now I understand why Paul came back to talk with me. Now I understand why he was so forceful in telling me what Ruth had told him." Simon pauses in thought and gives a hint of a smile before he continues, "I even asked Paul if he wanted to speak to Joseph and Paul looked at me with eyes sharper than a sword and said, 'I would not dignify this vile man with one word from my mouth. He has ruined this decent woman's life forever and should be banned from any place of honor forever more'"

Hannah looks at Simon, who steps forward to give her a warm, embracing hug, then releases her and looks into her eyes with a smile, "I can't wait to look at your mother and ask her forgiveness on behalf of the village. She has truly earned the respect and honor of everyone in the village."

With that, they start to walk again, both being quiet and simply gathering all that has been said. Hannah, realizing for the first time what a truly remarkable and courageous woman her mother was, while Simon was deep in humility for having been a part of a village that had treaded this woman so wrongly.

As they get to the home, Hannah tells Simon that her mother is likely resting inside and to go ahead and go start while she puts the cart away and gets the goats in for the evening. She rushes through her chores so she can hurry inside to see her mother's face as Simon explains everything to her.

When she gets inside, she finds Simon on his knees next to Ruth, holding her hand with tears flowing from his eyes.

"Mother?"

Simon looks up at Hannah, "I'm so sorry Hannah."

Hannah runs to her mothers side and feels her cold skin. She clearly had passed away earlier in the day, probably shortly after Hannah had left for the village.

Ruth looked peaceful as Simon and Hannah agreed that she had not suffered and likely just passed away in her sleep.

Hannah looks at Simon, "She never got to hear the good news." she said with sadness.

"I'm sure she did, Hannah. I wanted so badly to see the look in her eyes when I told her how sorry we were for treating her so bad. I will forever regret not having that opportunity. But I guess God was the one who held your mother in his arms as he showed her the conversation on the road we were having. She is at peace now, Hannah, and we all will miss her."

After a brief time of quietly holding Ruth's hands, Simon tells Hannah that it will be dark soon and he must go prepare a place of burial next to Saul's while Hannah prepares her body.

It is a quiet evening, as Simon and Hannah have a proper and respectful burial for Ruth. Simple prayers of gratitude and reflections of a woman who lived so much of her life in harsh judgement of a lifestyle she never had.

They both sat outside for the better part of the evening talking and sharing stories. Simon assured Hannah that she would now be the owner of the land with the goats and garden. They discussed the possibility of getting someone to help Hannah and Simon even promised to send out a young man and wife who were new to the area and looking for a place to stay and work.

Hannah liked the idea and Simon said he would send out some workers when he got back to the village to build a separate home for the couple so Hannah could remain in her own home.

By the next morning, Hannah was feeling much better. She was sad, of course, but felt that her life would be okay and for the first time understood that she would have the full support of the village as she created her new life with a young couple she hadn't met yet.

As Simon headed back to the village, Hannah started on her routine of milking the goats and getting them out to graze the hillside. She spent more time on the hillside than normal as she reflected on all that had occurred. She prayed some, but mostly just reflected on her mother and what a great woman she was. She was completely committed to spending her life honoring her mother by providing the best products to the village and giving hugs to any and all who welcomed her.

As the mid-day Sun made her casual day of being with her goats on the hillside a bit uncomfortable, Hannah decides to head back to her home for some refreshments and shade. She walks inside and freezes as she finds herself standing before a man with no expression but evil eyes.

"Joseph!"

Part II

Building God's Army of Love

7

———

Welcome

"I'm so sorry, Hannah. You're safe now." says the man holding Hannah in a warm embrace.

As Hannah opens her eyes, she shakes in fear and looks at the man, "Who are you?"

"It's okay, Hannah, I'm God. I wanted to be here when you crossed over to this side."

Hannah looks at God and is filled with a peace and even though she is uncertain of where she is or what just happened, she has a keen sense of peace in knowing that it will be okay.

"I know that everything was going well for you and the future looked so rich with love. Sadly, it only takes one hateful heart to ruin so many hearts of love. I am here to give you comfort and make sure you are in the right spirit as we move forward." God says in a warm and gentle tone that helps Hannah relax.

"But what about my goats, and the couple that was to help me?"

God looks at Hannah with sadness, "You have free will, Hannah. I gave each human the brains to problem solve and the heart to consider the consequences. Joseph has chosen to let the lies control his heart and he will be held accountable for his actions. The village must choose the path it goes moving forward. I am here to assure you that your loving heart will be rewarded and that your future continues to grow in love."

"Where's mother?" Hannah asks.

"Your mother is well and will join you later. I promise you will have many opportunities to visit with your mother – and many others– but for now, I just wanted to be here to comfort you and let you know how grateful I am for the life you had." God pauses to give Hannah time to digest her new world.

"Can I see Jesus again?" she asks.

God laughs out loud, "Funny you should mention that, Hannah. I nearly took on the appearance of Jesus when I came to welcome you, but I thought it might confuse you more, so I just came as this old man. Most people think of God as an old man. I'm neither a man nor a woman, of course, I am a spirit. I take on an appearance that most benefits where I am."

"So when I was practicing hugs with Jesus, was that really you?" Hannah asks.

God smiles, "And thankfully, you never called anyone Mr. Grump!"

Hannah smiles as she begins to understand better.

"Well I didn't have many opportunities to call anyone Mr. Grump, you know."

"Oh Hannah, people are hard to change, trust me. You gave a lot of hugs and treats to the children and children are my best thing. Hopefully the love you showed them had roots in their hearts and those children will not grow up to be Mr. Grump or Ms. Grump, right?"

Hannah smiles as she recalls the better times in the village.

"So where do I go from here?" she asks God.

"I wanted to be here when you came over to this side to say 'Thank You', as I did with your mother as well. You both were dealt pretty bad hands on the other side and suffered a great deal of un-warranted judgement, yet you both continued to love and pursue love in everything you did. I wanted to thank you personally and assure you that your rewards will be great on this side."

"Your guardian angel will come and spend some time with you explaining how this side works and what options you have. I have informed your guardian angel, as well as your mothers, that you and your mother can start your eternity by taking a nice vacation. There are so many things to see, places to go and adventures to experience. I want you and your mother to create a nice vacation for you two. Time means nothing on this side, so don't worry about that. You and your mother earned a nice vacation and I have instructed your angels to make sure you get the VIP treatment." God smiles Hannah seems even more confused.

"What's a vacation? And a V....I....P ....treatment?"

God laughs, "Well you didn't have any of that in the world you came from I know, but I assure you it's all really good stuff. Your angels will explain it all to you. I just wanted to meet you here and let you know how much I appreciate what you and your mother did for the sake of love."

At that moment, there is an angel next to God, "Ah, there she is. Hannah this is your guardian angel. She doesn't have a name, as she is only known as Hannah's Angel. She can answer any questions and explain everything to you from now on. It was a pleasure to meet you Hannah."

With that, God disappears as Hannah looks at her guardian angel who is smiling at her.

"Welcome Hannah. God is the ultimate definition of love, but he lives in several time zones and often says things that doesn't necessarily make any sense, but he just laughs and says that's why he created guardian angels- to interpret everything he says to people coming over to this side. I'll explain the vacation and VIP comments later, but first I will explain to you how this side works and what the possibilities are for you."

Hannah seems relaxed as her guardian angel begins to give her a complete overview of what she can expect on this side of life. Things are a lot different on this side from what she was use to on the other side. Time has no value and there is no physical consequences to begin with. In her work on the other side, time was important for her products and the physical requirements to keep her products fresh and appealing for her customers left her tired and sore almost every night when she laid to rest. On this side, it's your heart that dictates everything you do, so there is no limitations to making love grow.

Hannah becomes more excited with every word spoken from her guardian angel, and she appreciates how her angel enthusiastically transports her to various planets to give her samples of the exciting possibilities for her to explore. Her angel even takes her to a research center where Hannah will be able to search all the different adventures available to her. She can go back in time, or forward in time because time has no value, so there is no reason to rush your adventures at all. It's an exciting world she has come to and with each word her angel says, Hannah is becoming more thankful that this side is an eternity as the limited samples from her angel has given her a million ideas of adventures she wants to explore. She can only imagine the ideas that will be created as she gets more accustomed to this new world of hers.

The only rule seems to be that she can not go back home. The only thing you bring from your past life is the lessons of love in your heart, and you build your eternity from that.

"Well Hannah, I could show you a lot more, but I think it's time to get you started on your vacation that God wants for you." says Hannah's angel, "God has created two types of planets in his universe. The first type of planets are called the 'Next Step' planets. They are for those who pass away from their world without enough love in their hearts to handle eternity with God. People like Joseph would certainly not come here. God doesn't want to see Joseph until he's gained enough love in his heart to warrant coming to this side, so when he dies, he'll go to a Next Step planet and take whatever love he has in his heart and be able to build on that love until there is enough love in his heart to warrant an eternity of God's love. It's okay with God because God is the ultimate creator and is happy to create as many Next Step planets as needed to win a heart. God will never lose a heart."

"The other type of planets are called 'Adventure Planets' and are designed for people like you who have come over to this side with enough love. These planets are full of opportunities to use your love to help others or to simply enjoy. I will take you to the research center where your mother is and the two of you can plan out your vacation. A vacation is when you and your mother can go explore the many worlds created from love and enjoy them without any assignments or obligations – you are simply there to explore and enjoy."

Hannah is ready to burst with excitement as she hears about her new world. She is excited that she will have this 'vacation' with her mother and that time doesn't matter on this side.

"Do you have any questions, Hannah?" her angel asks.

Hannah smiles broadly, "I'm sure I do, " then pauses, "So what's a 'VIP'?"

The guardian angel shakes her head with a hint of frustration, "Most of us angels think God says that to annoy us. God loves to tease us. In some worlds, VIP means Very Important Person. It's when a person gets special treatment and treated fancy like they're better than everyone else. We angels dislike the term very much because in our world every soul is a VIP and God knows that. God's always telling us to give people the VIP treatment, knowing full well that there is no other way for us. God get's tickled at his sense of humor."

Hannah is humored by the thought of God being such a warm spirit.

"Are you ready to go to the research center and plan a vacation with your mother?" asks the angel.

"You bet I am!" says Hannah as the angel holds her hands and they disappear, headed for a new world of vacations, love and adventures with Ruth.

~~~~~~~~~~

Hannah and her angel suddenly appear in a very large room. Hannah looks around and is not sure what she is looking at. She has never seen a room like this before, obviously, but there seems to be an odd sense of understanding on this side that simply accepts. Before she can ask any questions, though, she notices her mother sitting at a table and explodes with excitement, rushes over to Ruth and nearly knocks her over with a warm embrace.

"Mother! I've missed you so much!"

Hannah and Ruth's angels look at each other, fully aware that it might be a while before they can explain this resource center to them as they smile and let the reunion evolve and appreciate that there are no time limits on this side. Ruth and Hannah are like two teenage girls talking about prom night as they are completely oblivious to their surroundings or the
~~~~~~~~~~

two angels patiently sitting next to them waiting for the two to get reacquainted.

The love of these two women is certainly obvious and the angels understand that these two didn't have a lot of moments like this during their struggles in the former life, so they are happy to let the moment develop without any attempt to wrap it up.

As Hannah gives her mother yet another warm, embracing hug, she opens her eyes and notices Ruth's angel quietly sitting next to her with a big smile and then realizes that her and her mother are not alone.

"Oh, sorry. We seem to have lost track of where we are. It's just so good to be with mother again." says Hannah in a most apologetic manner.

Ruth's angel shakes her head, "No worries, Hannah. That's why God made this side eternal. God never wants us to rush reunions of loving hearts."

As Ruth and Hannah gather themselves, the two angels prepare to explain this new world to them.

"This will be your resource center. You both will be able to come here at any time to plan another adventure vacation or simply to talk with either one of us, as this is where the two of us will always be. If something comes up, either one of us can transport you here at any time without disrupting your adventure,…" as the other angel interrupts, "We'll just put your adventure on pause," she smiles, then looks to the other angel to continue, "Yes, we are connected to your hearts, so we'll be with you throughout your eternity, but if we need to talk, we can transport you here for that." the angel pauses to let this sink in before the other angel takes over.

"This resource center has information on everything God has created in the Adventure Planets network and it's so cool to spend time here planning out your vacations. Everything you can imagine is in the adventure planet network. You'll be so thankful that time means nothing on this side, that's for sure." says the over-enthusiastic angel of Hannah before Ruth's angel picks up the conversation.

"You'll probably like to spend some time here reviewing the many possibilities, but before you do, let us explain a few things." she pauses again as Hannah and Ruth are totally tuned into every word.

"On this side, you will have an instant awareness of things that are totally foreign to you," as the other angel interrupts. "There are so many cool things you'll be able to experience that were not even close to being invented in the world you just came from, but don't let it scare you. You'll have instant understanding of everything and be able to adapt without any problem!" says the angel with an addictive dose of enthusiasm, as the other angel continues.

"Yes, you'll have a good understand, but we'll always be here as well to explain and answer any questions too." says the other angel before Hannah's angel interrupts again.

"There's a really cool place called Bauch that is so much fun...." as Ruth's angel puts a hand on her arm to get her attention and stop her.

"What?" Hannah's angel says to Ruth's, who is looking at

her with a stern expression, "I'm just so happy that they are on this side now. They both had such a crappy experience in their world and yet they always maintained the love in their hearts. I just can't wait for them to experience all the love and beauty of this side that they so richly deserve!" she says, as the angels turn and look at Hannah sitting there with eyebrows raised and a smile locked on her face, a bit overwhelmed by the enthusiasm of her angel.

"We are all very happy to have you here and look forward to seeing you both create an eternity full of God's love." she looks at Hannah's angel, then back at Ruth and Hannah, "Some are a bit more expressive than others, but we are all happy to have you here." she says as she looks back at Hannah's angel who sits back with her arms crossed in an unapologetic manner, before she continues.

"There are many options for us to start with. We like to start everyone in an adventure that is best suited not only to help you relax and enjoy this new world you have come to, but that also gives you a good understanding of what the possibilities are on this side." she says, "For some it means a family reunion where a person can spend some time with their family tree and the family members can explain a lot of the ins and outs of life on this side. For others, we may start with the world of service for those who simply want to utilize their God-given talent in helping others to grow in God's love. And for some like you – who have come from a world of great struggles and mistreatment, we like to start with a time of vacation. A time to relax and enjoy the many fruits of love that you were denied in your previous life."

Hannah and Ruth are soaking this all in as the angels take a break before Hanna's angel pulls up a screen from the table which has a picture of both Ruth and Hannah which appears to be a selfie at a remote beach titled, 'Ruth and Hannah's Vacation', that they would have no idea about because they came from the time of Jesus and lived a life of struggle in a small village.

"We have put together a vacation itinerary that we both feel would be so awesome for you two. It's so exciting that I can't wait for you both to get started," she says before Ruth's angel again puts her hand on her arm to slow her down and take over.

"We have designed a vacation that will not only be relaxing and a time to enjoy the many possibilities of this new eternity, but we also wanted to give you experiences that would help you understand the many new worlds that have evolved from the world you were familiar with in your previous life. For example, in your previous world, you and Hannah didn't read or write as that was mostly for the privileged and elites. But on this side, you'll have an understanding of the written word and complete comprehension of what you read. There is a lot of things that you will understand on this side that had no place in the world you came from. We want you to embrace everything and become comfortable in this new world so you can utilize your eternity in a more productive manner." the angel takes a breather to let this sink in a bit before she continues.

"The ultimate goal of everyone on this side is to increase God's love. We design a unique eternity for everyone that will continue to increase the love in their heart. God is love, so by doing whatever we can do to increase the love in each individuals heart, we are moving each individual closer and closer to God until they become perfect love."

The angels sit back as Ruth and Hannah look at each other with expressions of complete understanding and excitement. Hannah's angel takes up the discussion.

"Watch the screen here and you'll see what we came up with for your vacation. It's a general itinerary that will give you an overview that you will be able to change or add to as you become more acclimated to your surroundings, but for now, just watch this video and we'll have time afterwards for any questions before you both head out on your vacation!" she says with an overdose of excitement, as she starts the video.

The video starts with some light, bright bouncy music as a voice comes on, "Hannah and Ruth, are you ready to take your vacation?" as a very attractive woman dressed in quite revealing attire, they think, opens a curtain as what appears to be several people they cannot see start cooing oooohs and ahhhhs and clapping excitedly.

Ruth and Hannah look to each other a bit bewildered and shrug their shoulders, before turning their attention back to the video. Ruth and Hannah watch the video with absolute focus on every word and picture. There is nothing that reflects the world they came from, but there is a feeling of excitement in understanding everything that is presented to them, as foreign as it may be.

As the video wraps up, Ruth's angel asks if they have any questions. Of course the look on their faces indicates they probably have a million questions, but also reflects a keen sense of excited anticipation that tells the angel that they likely will answer all their questions as they get fully immersed into their vacation.

"Just remember that we are both connected to your hearts. If at any time we feel you are confused or uncertain about something you are doing, either one of us can pause the vacation and have you back here to make sure you are okay before moving on."

Ruth and Hannah nod in understanding.

"You guys ready for an awesome vacation?!" says Hannah's angel as the two shake their heads in excitement, and the angel snaps the screen closed as Ruth and Hannah begin their vacation.

8

———

Vacation Time

Ruth and Hannah find themselves in a world unlike any other they new before.

They are on a tropical island with beautiful white sand beaches, deep blue ocean waves and rich green palm leaves dancing in the ocean breeze. This is a very touristy setting that they never experienced before in their former life, but somehow, they feel comfortable and relaxed in the setting. As a man delivers some tropical, umbrella drinks to them, they look at each other and smile.

"When Jesus said heaven would be special for those who suffered unjustly, he wasn't kidding, right?" says Ruth to her daughter.

Hannah laughs, "I'm glad time has no place here because it's going to take some time to get use to how things are in this new world. But you know, for some reason, I'm not hesitant here. I feel a real comfort in my heart that if we just stay with it, we will understand everything."

"You're right, Hannah. I feel the same way. I trust that our angels know what's best for us and they are the ones who created this vacation. I feel the same as you in that if we just stay with this and enjoy every moment, it will all make sense and help us understand this new world we have landed in. I mean this drink is way better than any water or goat milk we were use to having, don't you think?"

Hannah nearly spits out her drink as she bursts into laughter, "I know! What do you think it's made of?"

"I have no idea, but it sure is delicious." says Ruth as they both sit back in their lounge chairs and take in their surroundings.

They spend a good time just talking as mothers/daughters tend to do. With hearts full of love, the two start thinking about all the other places that were featured on the angels video and trying to decide where they will go next. On this side, they have complete recall, so they can take their time in reviewing the many places and adventures available to them and with time not being an issue, they don't feel any sense of urgency to make a decision.

As they sit back in their lounge chairs sipping on their umbrella drinks, they close their eyes and recall each adventure and explore the possibilities. It is so real in their minds that it's almost as if they are actually there, so they take their time. As they relax and review the many adventures, the enthusiasm starts to fade as Hannah becomes more and more quiet.

Ruth knows what's going on and smiles to herself. "I could

spend eternity on this beautiful beach, drinking these great drinks and watching adventures with you, right Hannah?" says Ruth, knowing what Hannah is feeling.

After a pause, Hannah sits up, looks over to her mother, "No mother. There's something missing in all this." she says, "It's nice being here with you of course, but it just seems like it's all about receiving love. I want to feel that feeling I had when Jesus taught me to give hugs to the villagers and tell them to have a nice day."

Ruth smiles as she too sits up and takes Hannah's hand, "Your heart serves you well, Hannah. Your understanding of love is key to making your eternity a benefit for you and God. I must go back to my eternity now, but I promise, we will have many more of theses vacations. But first, you must go back to the resource center and develop your own eternity."

As they hug, Hannah suddenly finds herself back in the resource center sitting across from her angel and God, who are both smiling.

"You have a good heart, Hannah." says God, "We start everyone off with a great vacation and they are welcome to enjoy their vacation for as long as they wish. Most who come to this side deserve to receive a lot of love, so I am never concerned with how long they wish to explore the many possibilities and adventures." God pauses and smiles, "But you didn't even last one drink?"

Hannah hesitates but speaks with confidence, "It was a very nice place, and certainly being with mother was great, but I really think when you just receive love, you're not getting the best love. I really believe that it's when you give love, you receive the best love. I want the kind of love that I feel when I make others happy with a hug or a friendly greeting, or by making the best products they can enjoy. That's the love that makes your heart smile."

""Hannah, as you know, it takes a lot of people a long time to understand love. Everyone wants love, but it takes most people a long time to understand you receive the best love after you give love. If I gave you seeds and you held them in your hand, you would never receive the fruit of the vine. You must learn to give the seeds to the soil and let nature create the vine that will give you the fruit.. A lot of people hold onto their seeds of love and get frustrated because they never enjoy the fruits of love. But you understood even as a child and that's why Jesus was so happy to teach you about love. It wasn't the words that Jesus spoke that converted the villagers, it was seeing you and your mother putting those words into action with hugs and words of kindness, even under the worst of circumstances of being falsely accused of killing Saul, that made them understand love."

God takes a break to let this soak in before he continues.

"That's what I need, Hannah. I need spirits on this side that can plant the seeds of love, not hold onto them. I need love to produce fruit and teach other souls the magic of giving love. I have talked to your guardian angel and, if I may say so myself, I think I came up with a program that you would be excellent for." God pauses, smiles at Hannah and seems almost at a bursting point of enthusiasm. "I want to build an army with you. I call it Hannah's Huggers," God pauses in excitement, "This army will only be for children," he looks at Hannah with a smile, "Children are just the best thing I have created, you know." then continues, "These children will be recruited, each with a special mission to give a hug to someone in their world who is in a critical moment in their life and needs a hug. I have explained all the details to your angel, but I wanted to let you know how excited I am to get this program going. I just know that once you get going, you're going to have so much joy working with these children and planting the seeds of love in the hearts of those in need. You'll be welcome to take a vacation at any time, of course, but knowing your heart as I do, I suspect once you get into this program, you'll want this to last forever, " he laughs, "Which it will!! That's why I called it eternity!" God takes a break to let Hannah process all the information.

God's excitement is quite contagious as Hannah seems very excited even though she's not entirely clear of what she's getting into, so she simply smiles and says, "Okay" God claps his hands in celebration, "Great! I'll leave you two to go over all the details, and if you have any questions at all, I'm sure your angel will be able to answer everything." he pauses and takes Hannah's hands, "Hannah, you're going to have a great time with this, and I want you to know how thankful I am to have you on this side working for me."

He looks at Hannah, whose eyebrows appear to be bursting above her forehead with cautious hesitancy as God wraps up, "Hannah's Huggers. Now that's an army I'm going to enjoy!" With that, God disappears, leaving Hannah, who appears exhausted even though she hasn't said anything, sitting across from her angel, who is smiling and giving the electric atmosphere of God's enthusiasm settle down a bit before she takes over the conversation.

"I must say, Hannah, that God is a little excited about this program. But to be fair, he really did create a great program that is going to be perfect for you."

"Okay," says Hannah, who seems much more relaxed and anxious to hear more about Hannah's Huggers.

"To begin, I'll share with you that God is always looking for programs that involve children. They really are his best recruits because adults tend to ask too many questions, become timid and afraid of their image…. Their faith is often not very impressive. But once children know they are helping God further love in their world, they go after it with the innocence of, well, children and God loves it. Always gets better results when he uses children."

Hannah smiles and agrees, "When it comes to loving one another, there really isn't a better example than children, that's for sure."

"Exactly. Now in Hannah's Huggers, God wanted to create a program where you and I will find situations of people who are in a critical crossroad in their life. There are many circumstances where a person may need a little nudge to get them to take action for love's sake. When we find those situations, we would then find a child who is in the path of the individual who gives good hugs – that shouldn't be hard to do as most children love to give hugs, right?"

"I've never known a child who didn't love to hug." says Hannah in agreement.

"So true. So you would visit this child at night while they are in bed. Once they understand that you are working for God and they are comfortable with you, then you explain that the next day you want them to go up to the individual, give them a hug and whisper in their ear a phrase that you and I will come up with. Make sure they understand to give them a hug, whisper the phrase in their ear and then just smile and walk away. They don't have to explain or understand the phrase, so just deliver the message and leave it to us to make it happen." the angel pauses to make sure Hannah is good before she continues, "That night, the individual will hear that exact phrase again, only in a situation that will trigger an emotional response in their heart. This will, hopefully, be the nudge they need to get them to take action for love. Once we know the outcome is secure, you can re-visit the child and tell them that their hug really made a difference, and encourage them to keep love in their heart and never be afraid to hug people."

Hannah thinks about all that is being said, and she's really liking the whole idea of it.

"Hannah's Huggers. That sounds like a pretty good army for love, I must admit." says Hannah. "I'm sure there are questions, but I do like the idea."

"Just remember on this side, you have a lot more

knowledge and understanding of every situation that will guide you to making the right comment to help each child you work with take comfort in what they do. It follows what Jesus said when he told people, 'you will know the truth and the truth will set you free.' We recruit these innocent children to tell the truth, and the individual will hear the message again and understand what they need to do to be set free of whatever it is that's holding them back."

"I can see how this would help a lot of people. What if they don't take action, though?" asks Hannah.

"People do live in a free will lifestyle, so of course, they could turn away. But when God was explaining the program to me, he said if you have an innocent child deliver the message of truth with a simple act of love like a hug, and then you hear the same message again that night in an emotionally fertile environment, it'd be hard to imagine anyone would turn around and walk away. That's why it's important that we choose situations just at the right time to make the truth have more impact. You and I have to believe that this is the perfect timing for the individual to be receptive to the truth."

"I like it." Hannah says, "Let's do this."

The angel pulls up the screen as Hannah and the angel begin reviewing cases to recruit children for an army for God's love named Hannah's Huggers.

9

———

Cindy's Hug

Ernest Wilson (Ernie) is a quiet man. Retired from his career as a factory mechanic. Ernie loved working on machines and there was no machine that he couldn't fix. A perfectionist who never missed a detail in any of the projects he took on, he also was a firm believer of everything being in it's proper place. His garage was spotlessly organized and clean, even though he spent so much of his time there.

He was the neighborhood fix-it guy who could often be found in his garage fixing a lawnmower or bicycle for one of the neighbors. A friendly old man who didn't say much.

He lived alone for the past three years after his wife, Barbara, passed away. They had a daughter, a nurse, who lived on the other side of town.

Ernie was a school bus driver who enjoyed his time with the kids, though he never made much of an effort to engage with them. Good morning.... have a good day .... do your homework ... listen to your teacher... was about all the conversation you would get from Ernie.

The children liked Ernie because he wasn't mean, but they were often too busy competing with each other for conversation time that they didn't pay much attention to the bus driver. An occasional, 'Have a nice day, Mr. Wilson' or the rare, 'Look, Mr. Wilson, I lost a tooth' was about all Ernie could expect, but that's how he liked it.

His life was quietly simple. He knew that being a perfectionist was good when he worked on machines, but he also understood it didn't make for being a good friend. He often wondered how his wife put up with him for so many years. It wasn't always easy for her living with a man who had such high expectations for everything to be in order.

His relationship with his daughter was always strained , and he knew it was mostly because he expected too much from her. He expected her to be perfect. He never let her just be a child.

After Barbara died, Ernie figured it was best that he stay pretty much to himself. Be a good neighbor, sure. Fix machines, absolutely. Let the children be children, of course. But Ernie never wanted to be around people for too long. Didn't go to church, neighborhood cookouts and always looked forward to holidays being over. Ernie was content with his simple life.

~~~~~~~~~~

"Cindy" says Hannah quietly as she sits at the end of Cindy's bed, shaking her foot.
~~~~~~~~~~

Cindy wakes up startled as Hannah scrambles to calm her. "Shhhhhhhh, it's okay Cindy, I just want to talk to you" says Hannah as Cindy covers her mouth with her hands to suppress her scream.

"Who are you?" she says through her hands.

"I'm Hannah. I work for God, and I need your help."

"You're an angel?"

"Well, no, I'm not an angel, but I do work with an angel."

"Are you a ghost?"

Hannah is taken back and uncomfortable with the conversation, "No, Cindy, I'm not a ghost, nor an angel. I come from heaven and I work for God."

Cindy seems confused but seems to accept what Hannah is telling her.

"Am I in trouble? Is God mad at me?" she says with a deep look of concern.

Hannah smiles, "Oh no, Cindy, God is happy with you and loves you very much. That's why he wants me to talk to you. God thinks you could help me out with a project I have."

Cindy sits back and studies Hannah for a moment.

"God wants me to help you with a project?" she says thoughtfully, "I'm pretty good at arts and grafts. Do you want me to make you a sign or a card or something?"

Hannah smiles and appreciates how Cindy is settling into this strange conversation with a woman who works for God but is not an angel or a ghost.

"No I don't need any of that, but I understand you give really good hugs."

Cindy's eyebrows elevate in surprise.

"God wants me to give you a hug? Don't they hug a lot in heaven?"

Hannah is tickled, "No, not a hug for me. I need you to give a hug to someone you know."

"Oh" says Cindy, "Is it Mommy or Daddy? I already give them a lot of hugs, but I'd be happy to hug them again."

Hannah is falling in love with this girl.

"No, but do you know Mr. Wilson, your bus driver?"

"Sure I do. He's a nice man. Does he need a hug?"

"He sure does, Cindy. "

"Is God mad at him?" Cindy says with concern.

"Oh no Cindy. God doesn't get mad at people. He gets disappointed at times when people choose to be mean when they could be nice, but he never really gets mad at people."

"I don't think Mr. Wilson is mean. He's a really nice man How come he needs a hug?"

"Well he is a very nice man, and I can't tell you everything, but I have a special assignment that I think you'd be perfect for." Hannah says with a hint of excitement.

"Okay," says Cindy who seems very interested.

"Tomorrow, when you are getting off the bus, I want you to ask Mr. Wilson if you can give him a hug, okay?"

"Okay"

"And when you hug him, I want you to whisper in his ear, 'She did everything she could', then get off the bus, okay?"

Now Cindy looks confused, "She did everything she could?"

"Yes, and get off the bus before he asks you any questions. He won't understand, just like you don't understand. But God needs Mr. Wilson to hear those exact words. Trust me, Cindy, it will all be good and I'll explain it all to you later on. Can you do that for me?"

Cindy hesitates, then shrugs, "I guess so. But why can't God whisper in Mr. Wilsons ear?"

"Well if God just whispered that message in Mr. Wilson's ear it would probably scare him a lot, don't you think? But if a sweet little girl on his bus gives him a hug and whispers that same message, he may not understand what you are talking about, but it won't scare him, right?"

Cindy giggles, "I hope not."

"Good. So do you think you can do this?" says Hannah looking seriously at Cindy.

"I guess so. Do I give him a hug when I get off the bus at school, or when I get off the bus later at home?"

"Let's do it when you get off the bus after school. He may not ask any questions then because he'll be anxious to get everyone home."

"Okay."

Hannah smiles, "Do you want to practice?"

Cindy giggles, "Practice?"

"Yes, right now. But let me explain something first. Only you can see or hear me, okay? You need to be quiet when we practice or your parents might hear you. I don't want you to get in trouble, okay?"

"Okay …. I'll be quiet."

Hannah gets up and grabs a small chair by Cindy's desk and moves it next to her bed and sits in it.

"Okay, pretend I'm Mr. Wilson and I just stopped at your house." as she mimics opening the bus door.

Cindy giggles and gets up, walks to Hannah, gives her a hug and says,'She…..." then covers her moth, "I forgot what I'm suppose to say!"

Hannah laughs, "First of all, you have to ask him first. It's always good manners to ask someone if you can give them a hug, okay? And when he says 'yes'" as Hannah gently touches Cindy's cheek, "Because who would refuse a hug from this precious face, right?" as Cindy giggles, "Then as you are hugging him, you whisper in his ear, 'She did everything she could', and then get off the bus. Got it?"

"Got it!."

"Good, let's try it again."

They get back to their positions as Hannah sits up and makes a stopping sound and pretends opening the door. Cindy walks up to her.

"Mr. Wilson, can I have a hug?" she asks.

Hannah turns to Cindy with a serious look and tries to sound manly, "Why, sure little girl." and holds out her arms.

Cindy embraces her and whispers, "She did everything she could." and turns and walks away.

Hannah pretends clapping as Cindy giggles.

"Perfect, Cindy. That's exactly how I want you to do it, okay. Do you think you can do it?"

Cindy nods positively as she heads back to bed.

"Excellent. I'll come back and visit you in a day or two and let you know how much you helped Mr Wilson, okay?"

"Okay."

Cindy pauses in thought before she asks Hannah, "What do I say if Mr. Wilson asks me why I said that to him?"

Hannah smiles, "Tell him the truth."

Cindy raises her eyebrows in fear, "The truth? He's not going to believe it if I tell him about tonight?"

"Perfect!" Hannah says with a big smile, "Just say, 'Some lady came down from heaven, woke me up and told me I needed to give you a hug and say that.' smile and leave it at that. He won't ask any more questions, I assure you."

Cindy covers her mouth with her hands in giggles, "Well he's not going to believe that."

Hannah smiles and gives Cindy a hug.

"Well you don't think God wants you to lie do you? Always tell the truth and God will work everything out for you, okay?"

With that another hug as Hannah tucks Cindy into bed, then disappears as Cindy thinks about the visit, yawns and settles into a peaceful rest again.

~~~~~~~~~~

The next day, Cindy goes about her normal routine at school. It was a good day and Cindy was her usual positive self around her teachers and friends. When school was over, Cindy climbed into the bus feeling both eager and anxious about her assignment. Luckily, she had written down the phrase she was suppose to say on her forearm so she wouldn't
~~~~~~~~~~

mess it up. After all, the message was from God, so she really had to make sure she got it right.

Cindy thought it was good that she was one of the last stops. Most of her friends had already got off the bus by the time Mr. Wilson got to her stop. She practiced the hug over and over again in her mind and thought about how her and Hannah had practiced it, too.

As Ernie opened the door, Cindy takes a deep breath and starts to make her way towards the front. When she gets to the front, she turns to Ernie and smiles.

"Mr. Wilson, can I give you a hug?" she asks politely.

Ernie smiles, "Of course you can, Cindy."

As she wraps her arms around him she whispers in his ear, "She did everything she could.", then she lets go and heads down the steps.

Ernie starts to say, "Who did…" but Cindy was off the bus already and turned to him.

"Have a nice night Mr. Wilson" and that was the end of it.

As Ernie was leaving, he thought, 'She did everything she could' … Must of been about something the kids were talking about. Ernie shook it off as he seldom pays much attention to what the kids talked about on the bus rides.

As Ernie gets home, he begins his usual routine of fixing himself his one cocktail before dinner and sit back to watch the evening news. He didn't watch TV much, but he always liked to watch the evening news to see what was going on outside of his little world. He might catch a ball game now and then, but for the most part, his evenings consisted of a cocktail with the evening news, supper and either reading a book or working out in his garage.

As he settles into his cocktail and news, there is a report of a local girl who got hit by a car when she was on her bicycle and died. A very tragic scene unfolds as Ernie pays close attention.

They interview a lady who is a nurse who lived close to the accident. She is very emotional as she looks into the camera and says, "I did everything I could" with tears streaming down her cheeks.

Ernie freezes and connects this nurse who is so upset that she couldn't save the girl, and Cindy's hug when she got off the bus.

For the next hour or so, Ernie sits in his chair numb to anything going on around him. He makes no attempt to turn the TV off, get dinner or do anything but sit there. "She did everything she could" plays over and over in his head, as the vision of the tearful nurse on TV takes hold of his heart.

He understands now.

He has no idea how Cindy knew, but he knew the reason for the message.

~~~~~~~~~~

"Susan?"

"Dad! How are you doing? Is everything okay?" says the surprised daughter who seldom gets a call from her dad.

"Could you come over?"

As Susan pulls into the driveway, Ernie puts a couple of cocktails on the dinning room table before he heads to get the
~~~~~~~~~~

door. When he opens the door, Susan can see that he's been crying – something she has never seen her Dad do before- and thinks it must be some bad news from a doctors visit.

Ernie gives Susan a big hug – another act that she was not accustomed to – and tells his daughter to come in.

"I fixed us a drink. I apologize if it's not what you drink."

As Susan sits down she asks, "Did you have a bad Doctor's report?"

Ernie raises his hand to stop her.

"No, nothing like that. Please just hear me out."

As they both sit down , Ernie looks away. Susan can see the tears in his eyes and the struggle in his face to find the right words.

"Susan, I owe you an apology." he says, as Susan tears up with a confused expression before he continues, "I realized today that I was holding you responsible for your mother's death."

"Dad!?"

Ernie holds his hand up to stop her.

"Please. (He pauses) I've lived my whole life with the thought that if something is broke, fix it. This made me a great mechanic, but it made me a lousy husband and father. (Pause) I don't know how your mother put up with me all those years. I loved her so much, yet I always demanded perfection. I was mad at you because your mother went to your hospital broken and you didn't fix her." he pauses in grief as tears begin to flow from Susan's eyes.

"I am so sorry, Susan. I realized that fixing machines is

one thing, but how difficult it must be to be a nurse and do everything that you can and still people die. I can't imagine the heart it takes to be a nurse. And the thought that your own dad was holding it against you that your mother died when in truth, you and the other staff did everything they could to save her. You don't ever have to forgive me, Susan, but today I learned that I have been a perfectionist in fixing broken machines, when I should have been fixing the broken relationships in my life."

They both get up and embrace in a tearful hug that neither wants to end.

As Susan calls her husband to let him know everything is okay, but she likely won't be home for awhile, if at all tonight, Ernie fixes another drink.

"I'm sorry, Susan, I only have the whiskey and coke."

Susan smiles, "It's perfect, Dad. I guess I got my sweet tooth from you. Mom always liked wine, but I'll take a good Jack 'n Coke any day."

As they go out on the back patio, they settle in for a magical night of a Dad and Daughter reconnecting. There are many tears, many laughs and many tears again.

It was during a quiet time as Susan went inside to make another drink that Ernie thought about the day. He felt as if a brick wall had been lifted off of his shoulders. He thought about the nurse on the TV . Then he thought again about Cindy and her hug.

When Susan comes back, Ernie mentions it, "You know it's odd, Susan. This all started with a girl on my bus. Cindy is her name. Nice kid, but I never talked to her. She asked if she could give me a hug, and I said sure. And while she was hugging me, she whispered in my ear, 'She did everything she could', and got off the bus. This girl knows nothing about me, yet it was that hug from this little girl that started this wonderful evening of reconnecting with my daughter."

Susan looks at her Dad with eyes full of love.

"Whatever started the evening, I'm so happy it happened."

They click their glasses in salute.

"I truly love you Susan."

~~~~~~~~~~

"Cindy…. Cindy, wake up" Hannah says as she shakes Cindy's foot.

This time there is no panic in Cindy as she jumps up and gives Hannah a big hug.

"Cindy, you did a great job. God wanted me to tell you how happy he is with you."

"Is Mr. Wilson going to be okay?"

"Oh, yes, Cindy. We could not have asked for a better result."

Hannah spends the time telling Cindy all that had taken place and how it all started with her hug. She told her of Mr. Wilsons daughter Susan and how the two of them were re-connected as father and daughter. Everything was going to be great, thanks to Cindy's hug.

"I'm really happy for Mr. Wilson," says Cindy, then she pauses, "Does this mean you're not going to visit me any more?" she says with a long face.
~~~~~~~~~~

"Well Cindy, I do have other assignments to take care of. There are a lot of people in this world who need a hug. I will certainly keep you in mind if there is anyone else around here who God needs to get a message to, but you can keep helping God out by being a good hugger and I'll try to get back and visit – and get a hug, of course- from time to time, I promise."

"Okay. Tell God I love him and thanks for letting me help you with your project."

With that Hannah is off and Cindy settles into another night of rest with a big smile.

~~~~~~~~~~

The next day was a great day at school for Cindy. She just seemed to glow in happiness, and there was nothing going on at school with her friends or teachers that would dampen her spirits.

As she got on the bus to go home she giggled and said, "Hi, Mr. Wilson." She could see that Mr. Wilson was in good spirits today and it gave her complete joy to know why.

As she was getting off at her stop, Mr. Wilson stops her.

"Cindy. When you gave me a hug yesterday, who made you say what you said to me?"

Cindy looks at Ernie very seriously, "This lady who works in heaven came down and woke me up and told me I had to give you a hug and say 'she did everything she could' and that's all" she says as she smiles.

Ernie looks at her, "An angel, huh?"

"No, Mr. Wilson, she said she wasn't an angel or a ghost. She just works with God."
~~~~~~~~~~

"I see." Ernie says a bit confused.

"Have a nice night Mr. Wilson …. and say hi to Susan for me."

"Will do," as he closes the door and then freezes and turns again to look at Cindy who is gleefully waving goodbye.

"Wait a minute…..

10

Jerry's Hug

Fred was a soccer coach for his community soccer league. He coached the young boys and girls, ages eight (U8) mixed league. He loved the kids, especially his daughter, Lucy, who was on the team.

Fred was a single parent ever since his wife passed away four years ago. He has managed to do well in making a normal life for Lucy and himself. He was pretty good at helping his wife out with the house chores and he really loved to cook, so even though he was a single dad, he never felt overwhelmed with any of the day to day issues a single parent faces. He had a good job that gave him lots of flexibility so he could give his daughter all the normal things her friends had.

He especially appreciated how Lucy loved to play soccer. It was the perfect outlet for him as he also loved soccer and was happy to spend the time working with the kids.

The only thing missing from Fred's life was a woman.

After his wife died, he really slipped back into a world of

being an introvert. He never was a guy who played the field. He didn't date much before he met his wife and always felt extremely lucky that she came into his life. He also knew that he was young enough and had every reason to think that love could always strike again, but he pushed those thoughts aside and refused to dwell on it much.

Fred was content with his life as it was. He never wanted people to feel sorry for him because he was a single dad. He knew that life wasn't fair and that there were many people who were dealt a bad hand. He had learned that the key was not to complain, but to play the hand you were dealt the best you can. Fred always played to win.

As time grew more distant between the happily married man and a single parent, Fred knew deep in his heart that it would be nice to have a woman in his life. He also knew he had no idea how to go about finding someone else. He looked at dating sites, but he just couldn't get into it. He wasn't much for the bar seen, especially with an eight year old daughter. And joining clubs and social events to find a woman seemed so lame to him. Fred was willing to just let life be what it was without trying to complicate it any more.

~~~~~~~~~~

"Jerry …. Jerry, wake up" says Hannah as she sits at the end of Jerry's bed shaking his foot.

Jerry wakes up and bursts into a roaring scream that Hannah was sure would wake the whole neighborhood. She quickly grabs Jerry in a hug and speaks into his ear.

"Jerry, Jerry, it's okay. You parents are coming and you
~~~~~~~~~~

need to know they can't see or hear me – only you can – so please just tell them you had a bad dream and get rid of them!"

She lets go of Jerry and stands back as his parents come rushing into his room.

"Jerry, Jerry, it's okay. Mommy and Daddy are here honey. It was just a bad dream. Everything is okay now." says the mother as she holds her son in a crushing embrace until he calms down (as well as her and her husband).

His dad looks around the room for any other possible reason for the scream, which of course, he could see nothing, which Jerry notices as his dad walked right by this lady and never saw her. Hannah was glad Jerry noticed.

As his mother tucks him back under his covers, Jerry is looking over towards the closet, where Hannah is standing motionless with her arms crossed, trying to figure out how to regroup on this assignment.

"Tell mommy what you were dreaming of, honey." his mother asks.

Jerry hesitates, then looks at his mother, "It was a snake shaking my foot, that's all." he says.

His mother gives him another hug and he glares at Hannah with a mean look, as she looks at Jerry in disappointment and says, "Snake? Really?", as Jerry notices his parents didn't hear her talking, which actually was the point of her talking in the first place.

"Well Jerry, the good news is that it's still too cold for any snakes to be out shaking kids feet, so you can be assured it was just a dream, son." says the dad with a tone of humorous relief.

"Do you want mommy to stay in here with you for a little bit, so you don't get scared?" the mother asks.

Hannah looks at Jerry with a strong sense of firmness, "No, you don't", as again Jerry notices his mom and dad cannot hear her.

Jerry shakes his head no, "That's okay. It was just a dream." he says, then looks directly at Hannah, "I'm sure the snake won't bother me any more tonight." he says as Hannah raises one eyebrow in quiet disagreement.

"Okay, honey. Get some sleep now. You have a big game tomorrow."

With that, the mother and father give Jerry a kiss on the forehead as they leave the room.

Jerry grabs a bat from behind his pillows as Hannah is gingerly makes her way back to Jerry's bed. When she gets there, Jerry takes a violent swing at Hannah's head but she just catches it with one hand, looks at Jerry with expressive curiosity.

"Woe, hold on there, buddy. If your parents can't see or hear me, what makes you think a bat can hurt me?"

Jerry has an angry face as he thinks of a response, "Who are you?" he whispers in a rather audible tone, as Hannah raises her finger to her lips.

"Shhhhhh, you need to be quiet because I'm sure your parents are listening." She waits to make sure he understands before she continues.

"If you put the bat back where it belongs, I would be happy to tell you anything you want." Hannah says in a very calm tone.

Jerry glares at her for a moment, then reluctantly slips his bat back behind his pillows and turns back, crosses his arms tight around his chest and glares at Hannah.

"Thank you…. My name is Hannah and I work for God." she says hoping this will start to melt his anger.

"God who?" he says angrily.

"God who?… The God who created everything, of course."

"You some kind of saint or something?"

"No Jerry, I came from heaven to see if you would like to help me with a project." she says with little confidence that he would understand.

"Why do you need my help? I don't do any magic."

Hannah takes a deep breath of frustration.

"Oh Jerry, children do a lot of magical things, but I'm not looking for a magician, I need someone who gives good hugs to help me out, and I understand you give great hugs to people." she says with a soft, gentle smile as she desperately tries to get Jerry on her side.

As Jerry studies her with his arms tightly crossed, Hannah can see that this isn't going to be nearly as easy as it was with Cindy, but decides to keep it simple and eventually, he should come around.

"I need you to give someone you know a nice hug, that's all." she says.

As Jerry continues to glare at her, she takes a deep breath and continues.

"You know coach Fred, right?"

Jerry doesn't want to give in, "Maybe." he says.

Hannah shakes her head in a humorous expression.

"Maybe? Keep in mind Jerry, that I came here from heaven and we know everyone's heart. I happen to know that you not only know coach Fred, but you love your soccer coach very much." she says.

"So what if I do?" Jerry says defensively.

Hannah takes another deep breath.

"Jerry, coach Fred is in a critical time and we have to get a message to him tomorrow. We need you to give coach Fred a hug tomorrow at the game and whisper in his ear, 'Pay Attention!' and that's all"

Jerry looks at Hannah confused.

"Pay Attention? He's the coach. He's the one who's suppose to be saying that to us. Why should I say that to him?"

"You'll have to trust me Jerry, but I promise you if you just do that for me, it's going to make a big difference in Fred's life."

Jerry seems to be thinking about it. He really did love coach Fred and his daughter too. Most of the reason he plays soccer is because Fred is the coach. He would do anything for coach Fred, but he's not too sure about this.

"I don't get it."

Hannah sees that Jerry is starting to come over to the idea

that she really means well and maybe he is starting to consider her offer.

"My job in heaven is to get really good children like you, who give excellent hugs, to help us with people who are in a critical time of their life. I can't explain everything that is going on with Fred, but if you trust me and do just as I say, I promise you it is going to make a big difference in Fred's life."

After a thoughtful pause, Jerry says, "So you just want me to give coach Fred a hug and tell him to pay attention? What do I tell him when he asks me what he needs to pay attention to?"

Hannah smiles, "Just look at him and say it again, 'Pay Attention!' and run out to the field and play your game."

Jerry perks up a bit, "Am I going to do something great in the game?" he asks with excitement.

"Oh no, Jerry, it's nothing like that," she says, then corrects her letdown, "Well I mean I'm not sure if you're going to do something great at the game. I'm sure you'll have a great game as usual, Jerry. But it's not about the game, it's something else. I'll let you know later on, but right now I just need you to give him a hug, say 'Pay Attention' and go play an awesome game."

Jerry seems to be considering the project, even though it sure would help if he knew what it was all about, that's for sure.

"Well it seems simple enough. And if it will help coach

Fred out, I guess I could do it." Jerry says with little confidence.

"Great. I know you can do it, Jerry. I'll be at the game if you need any help. Just remember that only you can see or hear me, so if I'm leaning against a tree and you run over and start talking to me, everyone else will be watching you talking to a tree, got it?"

"Got it."

"I'll let you get some rest now, but I'll be at the game tomorrow, so don't worry about it. You'll be great."

"Okay" he says hesitantly, still unsure if this is just part of his dream or actually real.

As Jerry settles into a restful sleep, Hannah smiles at Jerry, "Snake? I'm not a snake, either, got it?" as she returns to the resource center to talk with her angel.

"Are you sure we got the right child for the job?" she says to her angel who is calmly sitting at a table looking through a book about planet Bauch, titled: 'Bauch- the New IT Planet of the Milky Way'.

She looks up at Hannah, "Yea, Jerry?"

"Yes Jerry. I just came from there and I have no confidence that this kid's going to be much help to us. He called me a snake."

The angel smiles, recalling how much Hannah disliked snakes when she was a little girl on earth.

"Oh Hannah, Jerry's going to be great, you'll see."

"Great? He tried to kill me with a bat and woke up the entire neighborhood with a scream that would have made my ears bleed if I was still alive on the other side, for crying out loud."

The angel bursts into laughter.

"If you were still alive on the other side, you'd be over two thousand years old!" she says as she laughs and looks at Hannah who is ignoring the humorous comment and is waiting for an answer from her angel, who abruptly stops laughing.

"Well you probably scared him. It's not every day a child gets awakened in the middle of the night by one of God's Ambassadors of Love sitting at their feet, Ya know."

Hannah takes a deep breath, "I'm just not feeling it, that's all I'm saying."

"I am. He's going to do great. You better get back there, though, the game is going to start soon."

Hannah panics and starts to leave when she stops and turns back to her angel.

"Is that what I tell the kids when they ask me if I'm a ghost? … I'm an Ambassador of Love?"

The angel shrugs, "Whatever you want, Hannah. You're not an angel, you're not a saint, although everyone on this side could be considered a saint, so you're welcome to say that you are unless they're Catholic, then you might want to avoid any further confusion and just say you're a ghost …. you're not there to sell them a resume, Hannah, you just have to get kids to give people hugs. Whatever you want them to think you are is fine with us."

The angel smiles, as Hannah shakes her head realizing the

angel is right and she probably is over thinking this whole process, and turns back to leave.

~~~~~~~~~~

It's a beautiful day for a soccer game, as Hannah finds a nice quiet place away from the stands where Jerry can see her. The kids are warming up and going through their normal pregame routine as Hannah finds Jerry who seems to have a very serious game day face on as he warms up.

As all the players are called in to start the game, Hannah anxiously watches to see when or if Jerry follows through with his assignment. But she notices that Jerry has located her and has signaled to her that he sees her.

As the starting lineups heads to their positions, Jerry stops at coach Fred.

"Can I have a good luck hug, coach?"

The coach smiles and gives Jerry a hug as Jerry whispers in his ear, "Pay Attention"

As the coach releases him, he says, "Pay attention to what?"

As Jerry is running out to his position, he turns and points to the coach and says again, "Pay Attention!" and goes to his position as coach Fred waves him off with a laugh, thinking Jerry was mocking him for all the times he's yelling the same thing.

Jerry looks over to Hannah who is standing by a tree and holds up his hands and shrugs with an expression of, 'I tried'.

Hannah just waves in acknowledgment.

"Well at least he tried and he did say what we needed him
~~~~~~~~~~

to say, so we'll just have to see." says Hannah to herself as the game gets started.

Things go as expected with a bunch of eight year olds. A lot of back and forth kicking the ball without a lot of strategy other than if the ball comes your way, kick it.

Suddenly from the stands, someone screams, "PAY ATTENTION!"

Jerry turns and sees a woman he has never seen before standing at the top of the stands, then he looks to his coach and she screams again.

"PAY ATTENTION!"

This time the coach turns and sees the woman and freezes. He's never seen her before and is instantly intrigued by her spirit when all of a sudden, the rest of the crowd stands up and screams as Jerry gets a goal. Jerry raises his arms in victory as he turns to look at his coach, who is still looking at the lady in the stands. Jerry stops and as his teammates gather around him for hugs and celebration, he turns and looks at Hannah who knows that the coach missed Jerry's goal and innocently shrugs her shoulders and claps.

"Coach, You missed my goal!" Jerry says as he gets to the sideline.

Fred turns to Jerry, embarrassed, "I know buddy. I got distracted by that woman who was yelling, 'pay attention'. I'm sorry."

Jerry shakes his head, "And you were the only one who wasn't paying attention."

Fred laughs and bops Jerry on the head.

"Then I guess you'll just have to go out there and score another one for me, okay?"

Jerry smiles as he shakes his head and runs back to get into position. For the rest of the game, Fred is struggling to focus on the game as he finds himself often turning towards the stands to watch this woman of mystery who continues to scream, "Pay Attention!" She obviously has never watched eight year olds play soccer before, he thinks with a smile.

When the game is over and all the kids are heading to their families, Fred conveniently runs into the mystery lady.

"I don't think I've met you." he says with nerves of marshmallow anxiety.

"Hi. My name is Amy. I'm Jill's aunt. I hope I wasn't yelling too loud." she says with a hint of embarrassment, "I tend to get a little emotional at sporting events."

Fred laughs.

"I'm Fred. No problem. I think you saved my voice. If you're Jill's aunt, I usually yell at her twenty times a game to pay attention." he smiles. "Between you and me, I think she'd rather just look for lady bugs than play soccer, but she has fun and as long as she doesn't get clobbered, I'm okay with it."

Amy laughs, "I know. She can spend hours outside looking for lady bugs and butterflies."

"So do live here?" asks Fred who is clearly fighting off the desire to turn and run away as awkwardness and fear is consuming him inside.

"I just moved here three months ago."

"Great. If you need anyone to show you around town, let me know." he says trying to sound like Mr. Casual, but with not one ounce of confidence. Now he has panic joining his awkwardness and fear.

He sounds stupid.

He's being too obvious.

God, get me out of this.

"Your wife wouldn't mind?"

Oh my God, of course she thinks I'm married. Now she thinks I'm a jerk too.

"Oh, no … I mean my wife passed away four years ago."

Oh, great. Now I'm going to get a sympathy relationship.

"I'm so sorry Fred. I can't imagine how hard that must be."

So what do I say now?

Don't play the pitty party hand, buster!

God, I'm going to quit while I'm behind and just become a monk.

"It's okay. Lucy and I are fine, really."

Lucy runs up to her dad, "That was a good game wasn't it daddy?"

"It sure was luc…. This is Jill's aunt Amy."

Amy reaches out to shake Lucy's hand, Lucy comments.

"Jill doesn't like soccer that much, but we're best friends at school." she says as Jill joins the group.

"That was a good game today, Jill." says her aunt.

"Did you find any lady bugs out there?" asks the coach as Jill smiles.

"Naw. I think it's still too cold." she says.

"I guess I'll take this girl home so the lady bugs can relax. If the offer's still there, I'd love to have you show me around town."

"Or maybe you can come over some time for dinner. My dad's a great cook, ya know." says Lucy, who has often encouraged her dad to go out on dates and doesn't want to miss this opportunity.

"Lucy!" says Fred in embarrassment.

"That would be nice too, Lucy. I'm not a great cook, so maybe your dad could teach me a few things." says Amy, who is desperately trying not to laugh at how awkward and uncomfortable Fred is during this whole conversation.

"I'm really not that good, Amy. Lucy likes to make me sound a lot better than I am."

Amy gets her business card out of her purse.

"Here's my phone number and email. Don't be shy and make me wait too long, okay?"

Fred looks down at the card: Owner – World Computer Security Systems Inc. Then he looks up at Amy.

"I'm a computer nerd but I make a lot of money, make my own hours and have an office wherever I want it to be." says Amy with no apologies.

"Great." is all Fred can say, so Lucy finishes for him.

"I'll make sure he calls you soon Ms Amy."

~~~~~~~~~~

"Jerry…. Jerry, wake up" Jerry bolts up from his slumber but Hannah grabs his mouth before he screams. Both
~~~~~~~~~~

Hannah and Jerry stare at each other in frozen pause as Hannah hopes for a peaceful start to their conversation and Jerry gathers himself and gets his bearings. As the anxiety deflates in the air, Hannah smiles at Jerry.

"You sure are a deep sleeper, young man."

"Why do you have to come while I'm asleep?" he says sleepily.

"Because you are the only one who can see or hear me, so if I came any time during the day, people might think you were a strange boy who talks to invisible people, and we wouldn't want that now would we?" Hannah says in a calm tone, happily relieved that this conversation did not start with an emotional volcano like their first encounter.

"But I don't like it when you wake me up like that. It scares me." Jerry says with a grumpy face.

Hannah smiles, "I know you don't, Jerry, but keep in mind that I come from heaven. Do you remember what you felt like the other day when you woke up in the morning after my first visit?" Jerry thinks about it, "Not really."

Hannah smiles, "Exactly. You don't remember anything but our conversation because there was nothing out of the ordinary. You woke up well rested and even though you remembered my visit, there was no feeling of any lost time of sleep about it." she says with a smile, "I don't like to wake children up in the middle of the night, but I also know that because I'm from heaven, I have the ability to make sure that no matter how long we talk, you never lose any sleep and always wake up well rested and feeling good. Did you know, I even have the ability to fix your dreams?" she pauses as Jerry perks up. "If you are in the middle of a really cool dream, I can connect you back where you left off when I woke you up and you can continue with the dream as if I was never there." She says as Jerry displays a face of wonder. "Or if you're having a really bad, scary dream about snakes," she pauses and looks at Jerry with raised eyebrows, "Like a snake shaking your foot, I can just erase the whole thing and get you started on a dream that will help you rest much better."

"Wow…. That's so cool. Can you do that all the time?" he says as he really seems to be engaged in this whole conversation.

"There are a lot of things we can do in heaven, Jerry, but God only wants us to do just what is needed to make the project work and no more. God wants you to control your life, not heaven." she says.

Jerry thinks about it. "I don't understand how I control my life." he says with a confused look on his face.

"As you get older, you'll understand more, Jerry. The important thing is to understand that there are two parts of you that make you who you are. The first is in your brain," she taps Jerry's forehead gently with her finger. "It's in there. Your brain is where you learn a lot about life. That's why you go to school. Each year you learn more about science, math, sports, art and everything else. It's not important for you to become an expert at everything, it's only important that you try to learn about everything. That's where the other part of you comes in." She taps on his chest with her finger. "It's called your heart. It's emotions that tells you how you feel about things. It's important that you open your heart and understand how you feel about all these experiences in your life. How do you feel about science, math, music, sports. As you get older, it's going to be important for you to understand how you feel about the things you learn and see around you. You have to pay attention to your feelings in your heart, or all the knowledge in your brain will only make you smart, not happy."

Jerry hesitates in thought. "You mean like coach Fred didn't pay attention to my goal?" he says with a bit of a long face.

"That's a good example, Jerry. When I asked you to whisper 'Pay Attention' in the coaches ear, it wasn't about paying attention to you making a goal." she pauses as Jerry snaps into a confused face. "After Fred's wife passed away, he thought he would never be able to fall in love again. He thought that it would be him and Lucy for the rest of his life and he was kind of sad about that."

Hannah pauses to let Jerry understand before she continues.

"If you had not whispered 'pay attention' in his ear before the game, I promise you he would not have turned away from you making your goal to see the woman in the stands who was saying the very same thing. A good coach ignores everything the fans are yelling about, because they are focused on the players on the field and thinking about that.

It was because of your hug that he turned to look at this woman, and that's when his heart took over."

Hannah smiles at Jerry who seems to be warming up to her explanation.

"Jerry, that's why I came back tonight. I wanted to say thank you and let you know how much God appreciates you helping me out. Because of your hug, Fred and Amy are heading into a world of falling in love. Lucy may have a new mom – maybe even a new brother or sister in time." she smiles as Jerry smiles even bigger. "If you didn't give him that hug, he would have seen you make that goal, but would have also missed that opportunity to experience love again."

She puts her hand gently on his cheek, "Make no mistake about it, Jerry, that will always be the best goal you ever made."

Jerry smiles at Hannah, almost speechless as he understands how he really helped his coach out.

"So what do I do now?" he asks.

Hannah smiles. "I want you to go back to your dreams knowing I won't be bothering you any more. But Pay Attention," she says pointing at him sternly, but with a smile, "I don't want you to miss any of your goals, okay?"

Jerry smiles, "Okay" as he gives Hannah one more hug before she disappears and he settles back into his deep slumber.

~~~~~~~~~~

The next soccer game, Jerry is anxious to see how things
~~~~~~~~~~

are going with coach Fred. He notices that the coach seems much more upbeat and playful with the kids. He also notices that Amy is again in the stands, but this time sitting much closer than before. And Lucy seems to be more playful, too.

Jerry is feeling pretty good about his role in helping Hannah. There's still a lot that he doesn't understand, but he knows that everything Hannah talked to him about would make more sense as he grows up. He knows that as long as he pays attention to the feelings in his heart, he'll be okay.

Before the game starts, coach Fred talks to Jerry about the game plan. Just the usual strategy and pep talk kind of conversation. Jerry is ready to go and says with a smile, "This time pay attention when I make a goal." he says to the coach.

Fred laughs, "Okay, okay …. I said I was sorry."

As Jerry starts to run out and take his position, he turns back to the coach, "How's things with Amy?" he says

"Great, " says the coach, "Really good. Thanks for asking." he says.

As Jerry turns back to head away, the coach freezes, "Wait a minute," he turns to the young player standing next to him, "How does he know about Amy?" he asks.

The little girl looks at the coach and shrugs, "Who's Amy?" she says as the coach turns back at Jerry and the game starts.

11

Erica's Hug

Margaret Perry is the third grade teacher at a local elementary school. It's neither the best part of town, nor the worst, so Ms Perry had a good mix of children that represented all levels of the social spectrum.

The school was a nice school with a good reputation. The kind of reputation that the parents wanted for their children, but the rest of the community probably didn't know existed.

Ms. Perry was a good teacher. She loved teaching every subject – science, reading, math, history – but mostly she loved to encourage her children to explore every topic and don't be afraid to ask questions until you understand. Kids this age always had a lot of questions, and Ms. Perry was always happy to take the time to help them understand.

Lately, Ms. Perry had been a little pre-occupied with a cancer issue that the doctors thought they had removed in an operation over the Summer, but the last testing they did showed it was back and even more aggressive. She was scheduled for a CAT scan on Friday to see what was going on.

Ms. Perry lived alone. She was still fairly fresh from her college days and was just beginning to settle into her profession as a teacher when she learned about her cancer last year. She was too young with so much ahead of her that she faced her cancer with a strong determination to get it behind her. She was so excited at the beginning of this school year because she honestly felt that the cancer was gone and she could settle into a normal life again.

Now she had to go back on Friday to see what this next round was going to entail and her heart was heavy with fear and frustration. Mostly she worried about her children. If the news was bad or even not so good, she was afraid it would make her a bad teacher. Trying to teach the children to be excited about learning all that the world had to offer them while your personal health was offering very little was not an easy environment to teach in.

She tried to stay positive, both with her children and in her private times, but she knew that she was simply holding herself together until Friday.

~~~~~~~~~~

"Erica…. Erica, wake up…." says Hannah as she shakes Erica's foot.

Erica lifts her head and shakes the cobwebs of sleep away as she looks at Hannah.

"You're not my mom… what are you doing here?" she says in a fairly calm manner for nine year old.
~~~~~~~~~~

Hannah smiles – mostly at the calm start to this assignment – as she engages with Erica.

"No, I'm not your mother Erica. My name is Hannah and I have come from heaven to see if you could help me out."

Erica sits up in her bed and looks curiously at Hannah.

"You're from heaven and you need MY help?" she asks.

"Yes. I work with a lot of children when we have someone who is at a critical time in their life."

"I'm in a critical time of my life? I'm only in the third grade." Erica says a bit confused.

Hannah laughs, "No not you. Someone you know is in a critical time and I need you to help me help her out."

Erica studies Hannah before she responds any further.

"Where do you come from?"

"Heaven. I work with God. I guess my title would be Ambassador of Love. I'm not an angel, ghost or saint. I just help God by getting kids like you to give people who are in a critical time a hug to hopefully affect their outcome." Hannah says.

"Have you always worked for God?' asks Erica, a bit intrigued.

"Well no. A long, long time ago, I was a little girl like you, living here on Earth." says Hannah.

"Oh, you must have died then. How'd you die?" says Erica who is really plugged into the conversation.

"Well Erica, how I died doesn't matter here. When I died, God asked me if I wanted to help him out with a program that involves kids like you." Hannah says, hoping to push this conversation elsewhere.

"Grandma died last year. I really loved my Grandma. I've always wondered if it hurt when she died? Does it hurt?" Erica asks full of curiosity.

Hannah takes a deep breath. She's okay answering Erica's questions, of course, but she'd much rather move on to the reason she showed up at the end of her bed.

"Well a lot of it depends on how you die. But if you're talking about that exact moment when your heart stops beating and your life comes to an end, no, there is no pain. In fact, it's just the opposite. Your pain stops and you suddenly feel a great comfort of peace like a warm blanket being wrapped around you." as Hannah recalls, she is becoming more engaged with this conversation. "When you open your eyes, you realize that it's not a blanket, but it's God who is wrapped around you giving you the peace and comfort."

Erica is totally locked into every word Hannah says.

"God smiles a smile unlike any smile you have ever seen before and welcomes you."

"What does God look like?" Erica interrupts.

"Oh God is a spirit and can look like anything. God always takes on the appearance of how you see God when you think of him. God doesn't want to scare you, he wants you to be comfortable, so he'll take on whatever vision you have of God when you come to the other side."

Erica is excited. "I always think of God as a beautiful lady, is that okay?"

"Of course it is Erica. God is love, and you can see love in a beautiful lady, or butterflies, sunny days, a smile on a strangers face. Love will appear in every way your eyes look for love. God is a spirit. When I died, God was an old man with gentle, loving eyes. But I was raised to believe that God was this powerful man who punished people if they did bad things. But then I met a man who talked about God as a loving God who wants everyone to be happy. I could never shake that image of an old man, but at least my vision gave this old man eyes that were gentle and full of love. That's what I saw when I opened my eyes."

"Wow. So when Grandma died, she opened her eyes and saw God holding her and he looked like the person she saw when she said her prayers at night?"

"Exactly. And I'm certain that your Grandma felt the same peace and comfort as she looked at her God as I did when I opened my eyes." Hannah says.

Erica smiles a big smile. "I'm glad my Grandma didn't feel any pain. Does she do what you do?"

Hannah laughs. "I'm not sure what your Grandma does. But God always finds something for everyone to do that they really love to do. I really loved giving hugs when I was on your side, so God thought I might enjoy working with kids like you in helping others get close to God with hugs. He calls it Hannah's Army, and I just LOVE doing what I do. I'm sure he has your Grandma doing something that she really loves."

Erica sits back and takes it all in with a big smile.

As Hannah sees the break in questions, she jumps in to get this visit back to it's original purpose.

"So Erica, we might want to talk about why I'm here with you so you can get back to your rest." she says.

"Oh yeah, you want me to hug someone?"

"Yes. Ms. Perry, your teacher." Hannah says and waits for a reaction.

"Ms. Perry needs a hug?"

"Yes, but it's not just a hug. I want you to give her a hug tomorrow and whisper in her ear, 'Be a magician', and then leave."

"Be a magician?" Erica says with a face full of curiosity.

"Yes. I know your favorite time in school is when Ms Perry gets out her book of magic tricks, right?" Hannah says.

"I love it. Ms. Perry loves to show us magic tricks when we have free time and explains the tricks to us, too. She has a big book with lots of magic tricks. It's my favorite time of the day."

"I know that. And that's why I need you to walk up to her at the end of school, give her a hug and say, 'Be the Magician' and leave."

Erica pauses in thought, "Well, I always give Ms. Perry a hug when I leave school, so that won't be hard. And I'm not sure what saying 'Be the Magician' means, but I guess I could do that."

"Great. I promise I'll come back and explain everything to you afterwards, Erica, but trust me, this will be a huge outcome if we do it right, okay?"

"Okay Hannah, I'll do it." Erica says with confidence.

Hannah gives her a big hug and tells her to lay back down and get some rest.

"If you see Grandma, tell her I miss her." says Erica as she rolls to her side and closes her eyes as Hannah disappears.

~~~~~~~~~~

The next day was uneventful for Erica. She had a good day as she always seemed to have and was looking forward to her hug with Ms Perry. Everything went well and as the children were being dismissed to go to their buses, Ms Perry reminds the children that they will have a substitute teacher tomorrow and to be nice to her.

Erica stops at Ms. Perry's desk to give her a hug as she heads out, as she was known to do. This time as she gives her a hug, she whispers in her ear, "Be the Magician" and lets go with a smile.

"Well Erica, you have to go now and catch your bus," says Ms. Perry. "But I promise we'll do some magic next week when I'm back, okay?"

As Erica runs out to catch her bus, Ms. Perry straightens out her desk and prepares to leave as well.

Friday arrives and Margaret heads to the hospital to meet her Doctor and get the CAT scan done. She is obviously nervous, knowing that this day and the results of her test will
~~~~~~~~~~

determine what kind of weekend – and beyond – she has to deal with.

"Ms. Perry, good to see you." Dr. Gordon says as she walks into the lab. "How are you feeling today?"

"Outside of anxiety, fear and a doomsday mind set , I guess I'm doing fine," says Margaret.

Dr. Gordon laughs, as she takes Margaret's hands and looks at her. "I know you are, Margaret, but hopefully, we'll get some good news today and come up with an aggressive plan to get this cancer behind us, okay?" says the doctor.

She leads Margaret into the room with the CAT scan and introduces her to the nurse who is going to run the tests. In a few minutes, everyone is in their place and Margaret finds herself alone in this room with a big machine that will have the eyes to tell her doctor what the next step will be.

As the big machine carries Margaret through the camera tunnel, Margaret can only think of praying. "God, give me enough strength to handle whatever it is going on inside of me." is all she can say, over and over again. When the machine comes to rest, the nurse comes in to check on Margaret.

"Are you doing alright, Ms. Perry?"

Margaret nods yes, as the nurse continues.

"We need to make another pass through the tunnel to make sure we're getting everything, okay?" she says.

Margaret nods yes again but is a bit concerned. She knows how expensive these tests are and it seems unusual that they would just want to make another pass if there wasn't something going on.

As everyone takes their place, the test begins a second time as Margaret goes back to her prayers. "God, give me the strength to handle whatever it is they are looking at."

As the test concludes, the nurse comes in again and asks Margaret to sit up.

"Are you feeling okay, Ms. Perry?"

"Yes." Margaret says.

"You can get dressed now and then I'll be back to take you up to Dr. Gordon's office. She'll be with you after she checks a few things out okay?"

"Okay" says Margaret as the nurse leaves and Margaret gets her clothing back on.

The nurse shows up after what seemed to be a rather long time with a wheelchair and smiles.

"This is just house rules you understand." as Margaret gets up and smiles as she settles into the chair.

Margaret sits and waits in the doctors office with a million scenarios running through her mind. All the good news and all the bad news. It could be this or it could be that. If it's this, what am I going to tell the children, but if it's that, how am I going to handle it? Her brain couldn't keep up with all her questions.

"Ms. Perry." says the nurse as he holds the door open.

Margaret gets up and follows the nurse to Dr. Gordon's office. She is sitting at her desk looking over the pile of documents.

As she sits in a chair, she notices that the nurse sits in the chair next to her which makes her heart sink. It must be really bad news.

After a moment, Dr. Gordon, who is never one to beat around the bush, smiles at Margaret.

"You must be some kind of magician, Margaret." as she stands and turns on a light that show some pictures.

"This is the scan I showed you three weeks ago. You can see here on your kidney and here on your lungs the spots which are cancerous cells that gave us our concern."

She steps over and turns on another light with pictures.

"This is the scan we just took today. As you can see, the spots have disappeared like magic." she pauses and looks at Margaret who has her hand over her mouth and tears quickly escaping her eyes.

"Margaret, I can't make a plan of attack when there is nothing to attack," she smiles, as the nurse puts his arm around Margaret and hands her a box of tissue.

"That's why we did a second run, because we couldn't believe what we were seeing. But the second scan was just as clean."

Margaret has a complete emotional melt down. Of all the scenarios that were running through her mind, this was not one of them. She just stared at the pictures of her clean kidneys and lungs and was unable to say anything.

Dr. Gordon and the nurse let Margaret have as much time as she needed. It was a rare moment for the doctor to be a part of such a joyful test result, so she was in no hurry to rush the moment.

"Is there any explanation?" asks Margaret.

"I've been a doctor in this field for almost twenty years, and I've seen a lot of things that I couldn't explain. But to be honest, Margaret, with my experience in dealing with this type of cancer, I was expecting the odds to be seeing more dark spots and sitting here telling you how much time you had left. I never saw this coming."

Dr. Gordon schedules some blood tests and sets up a schedule for Margaret to come back every three weeks for blood tests and then another CAT scan in three months. If everything looks good, then Margaret will be considered cancer free and only need a check up once a year.

Needless to say, Margaret had a great weekend. She visited her mom and dad to tell them the good news as well as calling or getting together with other teachers who knew and celebrate with them.

But at night, when she hopelessly tried to get to sleep, she thought of Erica's hug. She couldn't wait until Monday to see Erica and find out what she meant when she told her to be the magician.

~~~~~~~~~~

Monday finally came and Margaret couldn't wait to get to school. It was a great weekend, to be sure, but she was anxious to begin her new life as a cancer free teacher. She was excited to give her full attention to the children without worrying about spots inside her trying to kill her. It was now
~~~~~~~~~~

all about the kids and she was going to be the best teacher these kids ever had.

Erica was also excited, even though she had no idea what she was excited about. She wondered if her hug would have any change in Ms. Perry. She hadn't heard from Hannah, so she figured it must not have done much.

As they started their day with the usual chit-chat, there was suddenly a lot of chaos outside in the halls.

Ms. Perry heard a gunshot and immediately told the children to get down under the tables quietly. She went over by the door to lock it, but before she got there, the door flew open and she was looking into the face of a young man with a gun. She grabbed a thick book next to her and absolutely walloped the man with a direct hit to his face.

As he fell back, his gun went off, hitting the ceiling as the kids started to scream. The man fell to the floor as Margaret kicked the gun, sliding it down the hall and pounced on the man, ready to wallop him again, when she noticed he was out cold. She froze as security and police rushed in to help.

One officer helped Margaret up as the others quickly secured the man in cuffs.

"Are you alright, mam?" asked the officer.

Margaret looked dazed as she looked down at her body and determined that she hadn't been shot.

"I guess so."

As the officer leads her back into her room and to her chair, he tells the children to stay where they were until they got an all clear. He looks at Margaret with amazement.

"That was pretty awesome what you did. Were you in the military or something?" he asks her.

Margaret looks at him and smiles. "No. I just wanted to have a really good day with the kids and I didn't want any interruptions." she says half dazed.

The officer starts to laugh as he looks at her and his radio gives out the all clear. He turns to the children and tells them they may come out from under the tables and gather their belongings and line up to go outside when they get the signal.

He looks back at Margaret, "What is your name, mam?"

"Margaret Perry"

He smiles. "My name is Bob Casey and if it's alright with you, I'm going to stay with you and your children until it's all over, okay?"

Margaret looks at him, "That'd be nice."as their eyes connect, she feels a sense of butterflies inside and thinks to herself, 'I know that's not cancer cells going off in there' as she realizes she is staring at the young officer and quickly turns away.

The rest of the day was full of organized chaos with teachers working with their children reuniting with their parents, first responders checking everything out and doing interviews of the day's events and media trying to get their stories.

As Margaret worked with getting her children safely with their parents an officer comes to her.

"Ms. Perry, is this the book you hit the man with?"

Margaret looks down at the book, 'A teachers Guide To Simple Magic', and smiles. "I believe it is, sir." she says.

The officer shakes his head and smiles, "That was some magic trick, Mam. We need to keep it for awhile as evidence, okay?"

"Okay" she says.

Erica comes to Ms Perry and gives her a big hug. Margaret gets on one knee and looks at Erica, "Erica, what did you mean when you told me to be the magician?" she asks her.

Erica shrugs her shoulders, "I don't know."

"Why did you say it, then?"

"A lady came from heaven and told me I needed to give you a hug and say that, so I did."

Margaret looks at Erica with a lot of uncertainty and a smile.

"An angel told you to say that?"

"No, she said she wasn't an angel or a saint, or a ghost. She was some kind of ambassador or something, who worked for God. She did say she use to live here though." says Erica.

"Did she go to this school?" asks Margaret.

"Oh no, Ms. Perry. She said she was a little girl like me a long, long time ago, that's all I know."

"I see. Well if you see her again, ask her what it all means, okay?"

"Sure Ms. Perry. Here comes my mom, can I go now."

"Of course, but not without a hug."

Erica gives Margaret a big hug and then runs off to

embrace her mom, leaving Margaret thinking about the last couple of days when she truly was the magician.

~~~~~~~~~~

"Wake up Erica…. wake up!" says Hannah as she shakes Erica's foot.

"Hannah, am I glad to see you!" says Erica as she bounces up from her sleep.

"Shhhhhhh, remember, your parents can't hear me but they can hear you, so be quiet, okay?"

"Okay. Ms. Perry wants me to ask you what you meant by her being the magician."

Hannah sits back and smiles. "Well look at the last couple of days Erica. Everyone is calling her a hero for what she did, and rightfully so."

"So you helped her stop that man?"

"No Erica, it was a lot more than just stopping that man. Ms. Perry had a medical issue she had to get tested on Friday – that's why she wasn't at school. We kinda made a few adjustments in her tests because we knew the school was in danger this week and we needed her to be ready without worrying about the cancer."

"Ms. Perry has cancer?" says Erica as Hannah realizes none of the kids knew.

"Well, don't say anything to the other children. She didn't want you kids worrying about her. But when she got the results of the tests on Friday, it reflected a little magic from heaven and Ms. Perry was declared cancer free. That put her in the perfect frame of mind to be ready for the gunman on
~~~~~~~~~~

Monday morning, which likely saved a lot of lives. And that's being a magician if you ask me. Just as you told her to be."

"Wow, that's amazing. Do you want me to tell her that?" Erica says.

"Well you don't think God wants you to tell lies, do you?"

"I suppose not. So Ms. Perry is going to be alright now?"

Hannah smiles. "Oh she'll be better than alright, Erica. Remember officer Casey?"

"Oh yea, some of my girlfriends thought he was cute." she looks at Hannah who has raised her eyebrows and has a big grin, as Erica drops her jaw.

"No way! Ms. Perry and Officer Casey?"

"Way." Hannah smiles.

Erica giggles then looks to Hannah.

"So are you done now?"

Hannah smiles.

"You did really well, Erica. God really appreciates how your hug started a lot of things to happen for Love. Now lay down and go to sleep. And Thank You for helping me out."

"Well I ever see you again?" asks Erica.

"I hope so, but then I have a lot of other children I have to go find to help me with other situations, so I'm not sure when or if I can get back to see you."

"That's okay, I know God can probably keep you really busy. There seems to be a lot of people in this world who needs hugs I guess."

"That's right, Erica. Don't ever let anyone tell you hugs

aren't important. Look at what your hug did for Ms Perry and your school. Hugs are always a good idea, so keep hugging, okay?"

Erica smiles, "Okay" as she lays down her head.

"If you see grandma, give her a hug for me, got it?"

"I would be happy to." she says as she tucks Erica in and disappears.

12

———

Lauren's Hug

Jarred Johnson is a rookie quarterback for an NFL team. First round draft choice, face of the franchise, Stanford graduate with a degree in science.

This kid has it all – smarts, looks, athletic ability.

Since his days as a youngster in Pop Warner, he has always been the star of the football team he played on. Everyone knew that when he finished up high school, he'd have his choice of colleges to play for. Everyone knew when he finished college he'd be an early draft choice in the NFL. He had a great arm, could run well, was physically perfect at 6'4", 254 lbs, and was a born leader. Most people figured Jarred would have a Hall of Fame football career then become a TV personality or possibly get into politics. He'd be a great President some day, most figured.

As he participated in the volunteer off season camps, the coaches could see they made the right choice picking Jarred. He quickly learned the team's offense and showed good poise in the huddle. He was a good teammate as he brought out the best of the other players.

The team was optimistic as they approached the new season. Not only did they have a franchise quarterback, but through free agency and other draft choices, they had built a core group of young talent that could turn things around for the franchise if they all played to their abilities.

Jarred was excited about his new career. He loved the city and was overwhelmed at how he never had to pay for meals or drinks wherever he went. He signed a contract that made him an instant millionaire, yet he was finding it hard to spend money. Even when he wanted to buy a new car, the dealership not only gave him the car, but also paid him more money to do a few commercials as their spokesman.

Life was good for Jarred Johnson.

But there was one issue that was always there to hold him back from being completely happy. A tiny corner of his heart that he knew was there. He never talked about it. He didn't dwell on it. But it was there and he knew it.

~~~~~~~~~~

"Lauren …. Lauren, wake up." Hannah says as she shakes Lauren's foot gently.

Lauren moans with her eyes closed, "I don't want to get up yet." she says.

"No Lauren, I'm not your mother, I'm Hannah from heaven and I need to talk to you."

Lauren opens one eye and turns her head slightly to see
~~~~~~~~~~

Hannah, then turns and looks at her clock that shows 2:30AM, then turns back to Hannah.

"Tell heaven I'll volunteer for hell if you leave me alone so I can sleep." she says to Hannah as she drops her head on her pillow again.

Ah, teenagers, Hannah thinks. This is going to be a challenge, as she shakes Lauren's foot again.

"Lauren, please. I really do need to talk to you and I promise when you wake up in the morning, you'll feel well rested and in good spirits." Hannah says.

Lauren tries to ignore Hannah, but the foot shaking is getting annoying, so she flips on her back and sits up rubbing her eyes and takes a stern look at Hannah.

"What do you want!?"

"Shhhhhhh, Lauren, we don't want to wake up your parents now do we?" Hannah says with her finger to her lips.

"Maybe I do. How do I know you're from heaven and not just some nut case intruder?" says Lauren.

Hannah smiles. "Because an intruder could never scream like this," Hannah lets out a scream that has Lauren covering her ears with an expression of fear and pain all over her face, as Hannah stops, "without waking your parents," she pauses in silence with one hand to her ear to listen for Lauren's parents, then smiles.

"Nothing. Now if you want to scream like that and have your parents come in here, you're welcome to do so, but let me warn you, they can't see me either, so it probably wouldn't help you much. Or you can calmly talk with me and hear what I have to say, and then I can get you back to your precious sleeping." Hannah smiles at Lauren.

Lauren looks at Hannah as she considers her response, but has none and surrenders.

"So what do you want?" she says in a calm, quiet tone, which Hannah appreciates.

"I have a very special assignment that I need you to help me with." she says as she pauses.

Lauren looks at Hannah and shakes her head.

"You want me to help you with an assignment?" she chuckles as she lays back down and closes her eyes, "Go get someone else to do your work, I'm tired."

Hannah sits calmly and takes a deep breath. She's not concerned about Lauren's attitude – she's a teenager, and very good at it. But Hannah and her angel did a thorough review of Lauren before she came and Hannah knows that even though Lauren is a free spirited teenager, she does have a really good heart.

"You know, the good thing about living on the other side of life, is that I'm just a spirit, really, and have no lungs or any body parts that can limit me. I can do that scream like I did earlier and hold it indefinitely. I can even get way louder, want to see? Oh, I'm sorry, you're probably too tired and need your precious sleep."

Hannah pauses as Lauren pulls the covers over her head.

" Did you also know that when you come from heaven, you have the ability to play any instrument that you want, isn't that cool. I can show you. I can play this accordion

– a difficult instrument to master, I might add – like I've been playing it for years. I can do some really great polkas… listen…"

Laurens covers snap down from her head as she rolls over and sits back up with a look that could kill.

"What….. Do…. You…. Want from me?" she says, trying desperately not to explode and wake the whole neighborhood.

Hannah smiles.

"Thank you Lauren," she says as the accordion disappears. "I know we're getting off to a bad start, but please trust me. Another perk about being on the other side of life is that I have the ability to control the time. In heaven time has no value, so when I come to work with kids like you, I bring heavenly time – which has no value – to the conversation. You are welcome to look at your clock at any time during this conversation and it will always read 2:30." she pause as Lauren reaches over to pick up her clock which, indeed, still says 2:30AM, as Hannah continues. "And I also promise you that when we are done and you lay your head back down to sleep, I can make sure you have a deep, restful sleep and you'll wake up in the morning feeling great."

"Okay, Okay ….STOP!… So what are you talking about with this assignment?" says the impatient Lauren, who is absolutely unemotional.

"Well, I happen to know that you like football, right?"

"Right." she says with a sigh of frustration.

"And I'm guessing you have a crush on this young

Quarterback, Jarred Johnson as every other female in the city?"

Lauren perks up now, "I'm going to marry that man and have ten kids with him." says Lauren dreamily.

"Well that's not really the assignment, Lauren, but I know you're going to the last preseason game tomorrow and I need you to give him a hug for me." Hannah says.

Lauren's jaw drops. "I'll give him way more than a hug, I'll tell you that much." she says as Hannah gets a pained look on her face.

"Lauren, please, you're fourteen years old, for crying out loud."

Lauren interrupts, "Hey there's a lot of couples who have a gap in age. Besides, I know how to vacuum." says Lauren with a since of boasting.

"Well I'm sure that's what Jarred is looking for. Listen Lauren, I just need you to get down by the field during pre-game warmups and give Jarred a hug and whisper in his ear, 'Remember Plan B', and nothing more, got it?"

"I'm not going to say something stupid like that to the love of my life. That could ruin our relationship."

Hannah drops her head and takes a deep breath. "Lauren, you have no relationship with Jarred. He doesn't even know you."

"Well, if I whisper something stupid like 'remember plan B' on my first hug, I'll blow any chance of scoring with this guy, that's for sure." Lauren says with indignant thrust.

Hannah just looks at her. She is fighting the urge to abort

the whole assignment, but reminds herself that this is a fourteen year old teenager who is very good at being a fourteen year old teenager, which always requires a great deal of patience and gentleness. Maybe the best plan is not to argue with her but to play into her hand.

"I wouldn't be so sure, Lauren. If you knew what I know, you would see that there's a pretty good chance that if you do exactly what I say, I would not be surprised if Jarred Johnson is talking a lot about the young lady who gave him a hug the next few days or so."

"Oh.My.God. Do you really think so?"

"Well I don't have any powers to look into the future, but I do know that if you whisper in his ear, 'Remember Plan B' and leave it at that, it's going to have a big impact on Jarred, I promise you that." says Hannah as she braces for more.

Lauren thinks about it. "So at the very least, I get a hug, right?"

"Yes, Lauren. If you get down by the field before game time I can guarantee that you'll see Jarred and when you ask him if you can have a hug, he will say yes. That I can promise you."

"Well I suppose he'll never fall in love with me if I just sit up in our seats, right? This may be a turning point in my life, I would think."

Hannah rolls her eyes as the dreaminess from Lauren is a bit thick, but if it gets the job done, so be it.

"Ya never know, Lauren…. You never know."

Lauren dazes dreamily off into a romantic fantasy world,

as Hannah patiently sits with a numbed look and waits for Lauren to come back to Earth.

Suddenly, Lauren jumps up in a state of panic.

"Oh my god, I have to figure out what I'm going to wear … I don't want to be too obvious ….. something mature, but not too stuffy… classy, but not loud…."

"Woe, woe, woe, woe, Hold on there diva girl" Hannah holds Lauren's shoulders and gets her attention.

"It's still 2:30AM and it's just a preseason football game. I'm sure that jeans and a jersey would be perfect for the love of your life."

Lauren stares at Hannah in thought, then opens her eyes wide as if a brilliant idea just went off in her head.

"I'm going to iron my jersey so Jarred can see that I can iron, too!"

Hannah just goes with it.

"Perfect!"

Lauren jumps up and down clapping her hands, "Oh, this is going to be so much fun…."

Hannah gets her finger to her lips, "Shhhhhhh, Lauren, please. We can't wake up your parents."

Lauren clams up her shoulders with an ooops look on her face as she freezes and they both listen for any parents stirring, but it seems to be okay, so Lauren looks at Hannah and whispers, "This is going to be such a magical night!"

Hannah continues to go along for the ride.

"I'm sure it will be Lauren. But for now, you need to get back to bed so you can get your beauty sleep, right?"

Lauren looks seriously at Hannah.

"Oh my god, you're right. I don't want Jarred to see me with bags under my eyes, oh my god." she says as Hannah guides her back to her bed.

As Lauren climbs under the covers, Hannah asks, "You do remember the assignment, right?"

Lauren pauses and looks off into fantasy land.

"I'm going to give Jarred Johnson a hug."

Hannah waits for a moment, "And whisper in his ear?"

Lauren clutches her hands and holds them to her heart without losing her spot in fantasy land and says in a very passionate way, "Remember Plan B" and makes a dramatic sigh of love before she snaps back to reality and looks at Hannah.

"What the heck is Plan B?"

Hannah tucks her in, "Don't worry about plan B, I'll take care of that. You just do your part exactly how you just did it and enjoy the game."

As Lauren rolls over to her side with a sighing, "Ah Jarred, my love." Hannah shakes her head and simply says, "Sweet dreams, kiddo."

Lauren falls into a deep, peaceful rest as her clock shows 2:31 and Hannah disappears into the resource center.

Hannah points her a at her angel, "No more teenagers, got it!"

Her angel looks up from her book, smiles and blows Hannah's comment aside.

"Oh she'll be great, you'll see."

~~~~~~~~~~

It's game day and Lauren's father doesn't understand why his daughter is so excited about a preseason game. He's not complaining because she's in a really good mood and at fourteen, that's a great day no matter the reason.

"You're ironing your jersey for a preseason game?' he asks her a bit surprised that she even knew they had an iron.

Lauren tries to sound maturely logical.

"Well it's a new season Dad, and I wanted to get a fresh start and look my best for the team."

Her dad just nods, "I'm sure they appreciate that, Lauren."

During the preseason, it's usually just Lauren and her dad, as her mother would prefer to stay home and enjoy the peace and quiet. She's a football fan by marriage and only wants to go to the games when they count, and is always happy to give up her ticket if her husband has a friend who wants to go.

As they get to the stadium early for the tailgate party with their friends, Lauren heads for the stadium as soon as the gates open, which is not unusual as she often preferred to watch the teams warm up while her dad stayed back to hang out with his friends.

Lauren is nervous and giddy as she makes her way down to the corner near the home team tunnel, as that is the best place to get a high five, autograph, or in Laurens case, a hug. As the team wraps up their pre-game workout and heads back to the locker room, Lauren positions herself and makes sure everything is in perfect order.
~~~~~~~~~~

"Mr. Johnson, can I have a hug?" she says in a forceful, confident tone as Jarred approaches.

Jarred looks over to her and smiles. He gets asked for autographs many times and high fives a lot, but he doesn't recall anyone asking him for a hug.

As Jarred heads over to Lauren he says, "Of course little girl, I'd love a hug."

Lauren is appalled that he called her 'little girl', but she blows it off as she wraps her arms around him and melts, as she breaks the hug, she remembers that she needs to say something, so she looks at him and says, "Remember Plan B" Jarred looks confused.

"Plan B?"

Lauren smiles with a sigh, "Plan B" she says as she drifts into fantasy land as Jarred says a token, polite okay and heads back to the locker room.

Lauren nearly floats up to her seat as her dad shows up and the game time nears.

The game is uneventful for the most part, and for Lauren, it doesn't matter as she sits in her seat and dreamily watches her Jarred.

As the first quarter winds down there is a sudden gasp in the crowd followed by an eerie silence as everyone watches their prized rookie laying on the field in obviously extreme pain.

As medical personnel rush to the quarterback, everyone in the stands sits quietly still. Lauren has her hands to her mouth in horror with tears welling up in her eyes as she watches them bring a stretcher out to remove her fallen hero.

As the game starts up again, the air in the stands continues to be subdued. Football fans are use to seeing players getting carted off the field, but they also know what they saw, and the concern on all their faces reflect the reality that this could be bad news for the team.

The local news is abuzz with speculation, as there is no official word about Jarred. They only know he is at the hospital and they are running several tests to determine the extent of his injuries.

At the hospital, Doctors are combing over the ex-rays and discussing the best plan to help Jarred.

"There's no way to sugar coat this, people." says the doctor in charge, "We have to let them all know that there's a real possibility that Jarred may not play football again."

As the other doctors look at the ex-rays and nod in agreement, they go first to the team officials to let them know they will likely need to find another quarterback for their team. Then the doctor, team owner, GM and coach go to tell Jarred the bad news.

"So how many games do you think I'll miss?" asks Jarred when the doctor explains the injuries.

"I think at this point, Jarred, you need to start thinking about a plan B in your life. There is a remote chance, if everything goes perfectly, that you might play football again. But I think the odds are that you need to start thinking about other options than football. If we can get you to walk again without any difficulty, that would be our best outcome from what we see in the injuries."

As everyone leaves the room, Jarred is alone with his thoughts. He's never entered a football season without shoulder pads on, so this is new territory for him. As his medication kicks in, Jarred settles into a deep sleep, while the news gets out to the public that their team will have to look for a new quarterback and the city falls into a horrified hush of broken hearts.

The optimism for their beloved team is shattered like the hip of their fallen quarterback, and with opening day coming up this week, there are many sitting around numb at how quickly things have turned against them.

The next day is void of the usual water cooler excitement as the opening day conversations, normally filled with hope and optimism, is being replaced by quiet disbelief that most fans feel that the season is already over before the first snap.

At the hospital, Jarred's parents have arrived from their California home. They planed to come out early to take in their sons new city and have a relaxing week enjoying all the hype building to opening day. The itinerary has changed as they find themselves sitting on either side of the hospital bed quietly letting their son dictate the pace and subject of the conversations.

When Jarred gets to a point where he needs to be alone, his parents get up to leave, when his dad says, "It's going to be tough not watching you play football, son. But keep in mind you have a diploma you earned from a tough school like Stanford. Once the shock wears off, remember you have plenty of options."

With that, Jarred is left alone and asks the nurse to have no visitors for awhile. He starts to think about life without football. That phrase, 'Remember Plan B' that the little girl said and then the doctor, keeps rolling in his mind. He wondered why that girl said it. Did she know something? Was she an angel? It could not have been a mere coincident that she said the very same thing the doctor would say a few hours later.

Remember your plan B.

The more he thought about this, the more his heart grew. That tiny issue in the corner of his heart was starting to make itself known. As Jarred sat in his hospital bed thinking about this, he began to realize what it was all about.

He started to smile as it was all coming together. He remembered the missionary trip he took with other Stanford athletes a few Summers ago to Africa. They built a building for the school children there and he remembered how much he enjoyed it.

He also remembered that there were medical people there from a group called Doctors Without Borders. He spoke with a doctor named Elizabeth. She was from the states and he remembered sitting over lunch one day listening to her tell him about her experiences traveling all over the world doing very important medical work for those in desperate need.

He could see the passion in her eyes and when he left

Africa that Summer, he remembers thinking that if the football thing didn't work, he would love to do what Dr Elizabeth did.

The more he thought about it, the more excited he got. He was beginning to realize that he played football because everyone told him how good he was. He enjoyed playing football, of course, and all the attention it got him, but deep down in his heart he loved science. He was a rare college athlete who had no problem doing his school work. He realized that his fame and fortune of being a big shot quarterback had taken his passions into a remote corner of his heart.

He now realized what that girl meant when she said remember plan B. But he didn't know who she was or why she said it. It was all a mystery that he might never solve.

All he knew is that instead of working hard to get back on the football field, he was going to work even harder so he could be a doctor like Elizabeth.

<div align="center">~~~~~~~~~~</div>

"Lauren, get up, girl." says Hannah as she shakes Laurens foot.

As Lauren surfaces and realizes that Hannah is back, she sits up and looks at Hannah with eyes glaring in anger.

"I hate you!" she says, trying to keep her volume down. "You ruined my future husband's career." she says in contempt.

"I did no such thing, Lauren." says Hannah in a forceful tone. "I wasn't the one who tackled him. I had nothing to do with him getting hurt. All we wanted was for him to remember plan B, and if you watch his press conference tomorrow, you're going to see how important your hug was for Jarred."

Lauren perks up a bit.

"Do you think he'll mention me by name?" she says in a flash of excitement.

"Lauren, he doesn't KNOW your name. What's important here is that you understand how your hug made a difference. Because you said remember plan B, that phrase kept going over and over in his head until he finally remembered how much he wanted to be a doctor who helps under developed countries get the medical care they need. He may not of thought about it had you not given him that message."

Lauren draws her hands to her heart with a big sigh and dreamily says, "Isn't that just like my Jarred. In the face of absolute tragedy in his life, he still reaches out to help those poor children in desperate need of medical care. I am humbled by the heart of this great man."

Hannah looks as if she is about to throw up, but reminds herself that this is a teenager in love, and gathers herself together.

"Yes Lauren, he has a very nice heart, and we are all excited for him. Be sure and watch the press conference tomorrow and remember how much God appreciates you helping us out."

Lauren, still locked in her fantasy dreams somewhere,

replies, "It was my honor to help Jarred set the path that will save those poor forgotten children."

"Okay then. We need to lay down now and get some rest."

"Oh yes, Hannah. I have a lifetime of ministry ahead of me. I must be prepared for a life of struggle."

As Hannah tucks her in, she says, "well, I hope you don't hate me any more." Lauren looks at Hannah.

"Oh my dear sweet angel, you know the world has far too much hatred. We need to love one another."

Hannah takes a deep breath and smiles at Lauren.

"Okay, great then. I'll let you have your rest now. Thanks for helping us out, Lauren. It was truly a unique experience."

"Unique, Indeed, Hannah," as Lauren slips into a deep, peaceful rest, as Hannah returns to the research center.

~~~~~~~~~~

"No more teenagers, got it!?" Hannah says to her angel as she approaches the table.

"She did great, Hannah," as her angel looks up from her book.

"You did great. We had a positive outcome. Can't do better than that."

Hannah shakes her head, "Well, we were lucky. From now on ten years old or younger, okay?"

"Well Hannah some times we have to work with what we got, you know. Besides, I don't see what the fuss is all about. It worked out great." the angel pauses and smiles sheepishly to Hannah.
~~~~~~~~~~

"You know they're going to get married."

Hannah thinks she's making fun of Lauren, but then the look on the angel's face suggests she is not kidding.

"Excuse me?"

The angel smiles and shakes her head in confirmation.

"Ewwwwwwe… She's only fourteen, and a very good fourteen. He can do way better than that." says Hannah with a look of disgust.

"Well, he's not going to marry her now, Hannah," the angel pauses and looks at her, "Ten years from now, she'll be wrapping up nursing school and Jarred will come speak at a career day at the school. A much more mature Lauren will introduce herself after the talk and jokingly tell him what a crush she had on him back then. She'll also mention that she was at his last game and humorously mention that she at least got a hug before the game. Jarred's jaw drops and he says, 'you're the girl who told me to remember plan B' and, well, it get's real sappy after that, but I think you get the picture. It's actually kind of sweet how they fall in love and all."

Hannah looks pleasantly surprised and smiles before she gets a serious look at her angel.

"Wait a minute, how do you know this? We can't see into the future?"

"You can't see into the future because you're a dead human. Angels only exist in a world that has no calenders. We wouldn't be very good guardian angels if we couldn't see what was coming, ya know."

Hannah doesn't like the 'dead human' comment, but the rest of her comment makes sense.

"If you can see what's coming, how come you didn't stop Joseph from killing me?"

"That's why we don't like the term 'guardian' angel. It's not our job to guard you, it's our job to look over you. God gave you humans a free will. We can't change the will of anyone, we can only try to steer you to the right path. Even though angels don't really have emotions, I can assure you that Joseph's angel was pretty ticked off. After Joseph died, she told God her next assignment better be a decent fellow, that's for sure."

Hannah thinks about it all. She's learning more with each assignment, but the bottom line is that she really does love her heaven and working with the children.

"Ready for your next assignment, or do you need a vacation after working with a teenager?" says her angel with a smile.

"Ten or younger, I'll take it. If it's a teenager, I'm on vacation."

They both get a laugh as the angel responds.

"Well, I have a really good one here, and she's only eight."

13

——

Fatima's Hug

Abdul Raheem is the leader of a terrorist group in a small region of a third world country. Known for his absolutely relentless pursuit of his enemy, Abdul Raheem is one of the most wanted terrorists and most feared men in the world. You don't mess with Raheem. His followers are extremely loyal to him, as they have witnessed him kill many people without any hesitation.

He enjoyed his power. He enjoyed watching those against him crawl and beg for mercy. He especially enjoyed looking into their eyes just before he pulled the trigger to end their life.

This was a man of pure evil.

Abdul Raheem was always in hiding. Always on the move. He was very sophisticated in his ability to post videos on various web sites and had a rather large following of people outside of the small circle of men who were with him.

Many have tried. Many came close. But Abdul Raheem

was still a free man hiding out in remote areas, posting inflaming videos of hateful rhetoric, and mocking the civilized world for their inability to capture him. He was a ruthless leader. He would pilfer villages of everything of any value and use it to obtain food and ammunition. He always ate first and would only share after he had his fill. He was a very religious man, too. He made his followers maintain a strict code of obedience to the teachings of the Koran and would not tolerate any challenge to his teachings or rules. His way was the only way and your choice was to follow or die.

~~~~~~~~~~

"Fatima, it's okay. I won't hurt you." says Hannah to the little girl standing in the dark corner of a bombed out building in the middle of a village of ruins and smoldering timbers.

Fatima is an orphan now. Her mother, father and sister are buried in the rubble somewhere within the village along with most of the other villagers. Those who survived the attack have escaped, leaving Fatima alone.

She spends her days in hiding and searching for food. She is frail in appearance and filthy with only a tee shirt and pants to cover her.

"It's okay, Fatima, I come from heaven and am here to take you home." says Hannah who is almost overwhelmed with emotions as she looks into the eyes of this young girl. Her eyes reflect so much pain, so much fear and so much emptiness, yet Hannah easily sees that in a better world, this child would be beautiful and those same rich brown eyes
~~~~~~~~~~

would melt the heart of anyone lucky enough to behold them.

"I won't hurt you, Fatima. I want to help you."

It is obvious that Fatima has lost almost all of her ability to trust, as she is clearly not interested in accepting Hannah.

Hannah knew that this was going to be a tough assignment, but she also knew that it would be the most rewarding assignment she would ever have.

This distraught, sad little girl was going to be asked to perform a courageous act of love unlike any other act of love, and she would have to be brave and trusting of Hannah in order to have a positive outcome.

Hannah sits on a pile of rubble and smiles at Fatima, who has not budged from her corner.

"I want to help you, Fatima." she says with a smile of passion.

"Why do you want to help me?" asks Fatima without making any movement that would indicate her cooperation.

"Because I work for God and he wants me to help you do a job for him."

"Why would God want me to do a job for him?"

"Because you are the only person God trusts who can do the job right for him." Hannah says, being careful with every word, knowing how broken this girl is.

Fatima doesn't respond, but just looks at Hannah with those big brown eyes. Hannah can tell that Fatima is thinking, which is a good sign, but is in no hurry to rush.

"Why does God trust me?"

"Because God sees your heart, Fatima." Hannah says and pauses to give her every opportunity to ask more before she continues, "God knows that you have seen a lot of really bad things with your eyes. But God looks at everyone through their hearts, and he knows you have a heart full of love."

Fatima continues to look at Hannah and seems to take great caution before every response.

"I don't feel any love." she says.

"Of course you don't, Fatima. You feel sadness and emptiness because that's all the world has given you."

Fatima struggles to understand.

"Why does God let all this happen?"

"Because he promised to let everyone decide what they wanted their world to be."

"Why do they want the world to be like this?"

"Because there is a lot of people who have lost the love."

Fatima considers Hannah's comments. Of course, given the circumstances of the world around them, Hannah understands that these answers are not going to be satisfying to the young girl who has had so little experience with love in her short life.

"I don't like this world any more."

"I know Fatima. I'm going to take you to a better world soon, I promise. But first I want you to help me do this one job for God."

"Where are you going to take me?"

"To a place where your heart will only feel love."

"Will I see my sister?" Fatima says in hesitation.

"You miss your family don't you?" Hannah says with compassion. Fatima just nods.

"Where I take you, you will never miss your family again." Hannah says with an assuring smile.

"Why can't we go now?"

"Oh, we'll be going very soon, I promise, but first I need your help with this job."

"What job?"

Hannah knows she doesn't have a lot of time left, so she decides to push on.

"I understand you give really good hugs." Fatima shrugs.

"I don't feel like giving hugs much any more."

"I know you don't, Fatima. But this is going to be a very important hug that will help God out a lot."

"Who does he want me to hug?"

Hannah takes a deep breath, "There is a man coming to this village. He's almost here. He needs a hug."

Fatima hesitates in fear. Men coming to her village doesn't sound very good.

Hannah continues, "Fatima, I need you to be very, very brave. This is a mean man that is coming, and I need you to be strong for God and give this man a hug and whisper in his ear, 'God is Love' and then just look at him with those big beautiful eyes of yours and smile at him. It's going to be hard for you, I know, but I'll be standing right behind him and help you okay?"

Fatima is really not sure about this, but Hannah doesn't have time as she hears people coming up the road.

"Fatima, no one but you can see me or hear me, okay? I will be right with you and guide you every step of the way. I promise when we are done, I will take you to see your mother, father and sister and you'll never have to live in pain again, okay?"

Before Fatima has a chance to respond, a man shows up in the doorway and Fatima screams.

"Fatima, be still, I'm with you." Hannah says as the energy escalates as more men come into the building.

"It's okay Fatima, I'm with you. Be still and don't say anything yet."

Hannah can see Fatima's chest shaking in fear as the men stand there with guns staring at her.

Then Abdul Raheem walks in.

"Well, what do we have here?" says Raheem as he walks up to Fatima and gets down on one knee.

"What is your name, little one?"

Hannah positions herself directly behind him and looks at Fatima.

"Don't say anything, just look directly into his eyes."

Fatima nervously follows Hannah, which gives Hannah a feeling of confidence that Fatima is going to pull this off.

Raheem turns to his soldiers and says, "It looks like we have a shy one here." the soldiers smile as Raheem turns back to Fatima, "If you don't want to give me your name, that's okay, I'll call you little one." he says as the others laugh.

"Be still Fatima, you're doing great. I'm with you." says Hannah from directly behind Raheem.

"I'll protect you little one, if you come give Raheem a nice hug." says Raheem with a big untrustworthy smile.

"Perfect, Fatima, he's playing into our hand. Very slowly take a few steps up to him."

Hannah says as Fatima looks at her in hesitation.

"I know, honey, nobody wants to hug this guy, I know. You're doing great Fatima. Take another step slowly."

" Now carefully put your arms around him."

"Good."

"Now whisper in his ear 'God is Love'."

"God is Love" Fatima says

"Perfect. Now step back and stare at him."

Fatima takes a step back and looks at Raheem, who locks eyes with the girl.

"Perfect, Fatima, hold it right there and don't move a muscle."

Raheem seems to be lost for words.

"Hold it."

The glaring becomes a little uncomfortable.

"Okay, good Fatima."

"Now very slowly, I want you to start a smile."

"Very slowly, Fatima."

"That's it, good, you're doing great Fatima."

"Perfect, now hold that smile, Fatima."

"Hold it a little longer."

"It's reaching his heart, Fatima."

"Okay, you're good. Now I'm going to count to three and when I get to three, I want you to turn and run as fast as you can that way." Hannah points to the crumbled wall to the right of Fatima.

"One…. hold it."

"Two, Fatima, I'm so proud of you. You've done a great job."

"THREE!…..GO!"

Fatima turns and bolts out of the building through the crumbled wall as chaos and surprise takes over.

As Hannah's head drops, she hears gunfire outside.

~~~~~~~~~~

"It's okay, Fatima, you're safe now." says God as he holds Fatima in his arms.

Fatima looks up at him and starts to react in fear, but looking into God's eyes gives her a sense of calm that she has never felt before. She looks down and sees that she is no longer filthy and she can feel that she is clean and void of the hunger pains that have been with her.

"I know you are anxious to be with your family, but I just had to be here and tell you how happy I am for the job you and Hannah did for me." God says with a truly engaging smile.

Fatima looks around, then to God.

"Where is she?"

"You'll see Hannah again, I promise."

"What happened to that mean man?" Fatima asks with a scowl.

God smiles, "That mean old man is going to be alright, thanks to you. He's actually going to become one of my best
~~~~~~~~~~

Ambassadors of Love, and it's all because a filthy, hunger little girl like you gave him a hug. Isn't that fantastic?"

Fatima giggles as God looks at her.

God is so happy to see her like this. Full of giggles, clean and happy.

"How about we go look for your family. I know they're up here somewhere," God smiles.

"But if you're God, don't you know where everyone is?"

"Well, Fatima, I'm really good at love, but not so good at directions. Where do you think we could find your family?"

Fatima raises her eyebrows in disbelief that God, who created everything, would be asking her for directions in a place that she just arrived at and has no idea where to even start.

"I've never been here before." she says in protest. "They were sitting at the table eating when the noise started happening."

"Well that sounds like a good place to start, young lady," then God looks at her and smiles, "But I can do without that noise, right?"

Fatima shakes her head with a strong expression of agreement. God stands and takes Fatima's hand.

"Let's go then."

~~~~~~~~~~

"He's been acting really strange lately." says one of the soldiers.

"I know. He's not intimidating as he was before. It's like
~~~~~~~~~~

he's lost his edge or something." another soldier says in agreement.

Abdul Raheem has been in a constant battle ever since Fatima's hug.

Those words – God is Love- and those eyes staring at him keep coming into his focus.

He can't sleep.

His appetite is shot.

He finds it harder and harder to be the aggressive, intimidating powerful leader that his soldiers expect him to be. He wants to be left alone now and only gets upset when his quiet time is interrupted by one of his soldiers.

And his soldiers are noticing it more, too. He use to be very focused and confident as he moved from village to village, but lately, he just let's the soldiers do his dirty work without any effort to participate himself. He hasn't made a video since Fatima's hug and speculation is spreading swiftly that maybe the leader is dead.

He's confused.

He has feelings in his heart that he's never had before. It feels like his heart is beating in his throat and he constantly feels as if he could break into tears at any moment.

He tells his soldiers to lay low as he heads down the road to investigate the next village.

"Don't you want someone to come with you?" one of the soldiers asks.

"No, you all rest. When you hear me shoot off two rounds, you'll know the coast is clear and come then."

As he starts down the road, the soldiers look at each other bewildered. Raheem has never given such instructions. He always has them go into a village first before they signal him that it's clear.

As he walks down the road, he again thinks 'God is Love'.

His eyes begin to water.

'God is Love'

He realizes he has done nothing in his life that resembles love.

'God is Love'

He begins to see all of the faces of people he has killed.

'God is Love'

He sees the eyes of that little one as she smiles at him.

'God is Love'

He lets go of his rifle as tears begin to flow.

'God is Love'

He falls to his knees.

'God is Love'

He sees two figures walking up the road towards him.

'God is Love'

It appears to be a mother and her child.

'God is Love'

'God is Love'

'God is Love'

As Hannah and Fatima reach Raheem, he is overwhelmed with emotions.

"Little one …. You have saved my life."

Fatima steps up to Raheem and gives him a hug, then steps back and smiles at him.

"No …. We saved your heart."

Planes can be heard approaching and within seconds bullets and bombs start flying.

Hannah's Huggers

THE END

Current Status

HANNAH: Continues to visit children all over the world to recruit them to give hugs to people in a critical point in their life. If you are approached by a child who wants to give you a hug and they whisper something in your ear, please "PAY ATTENTION!"

RUTH: Ruth continues to be an Ambassador of Love, but she works with battered women who are in a critical point in their life. With God's frustration that the Bible only referred to Ruth as a woman at the well (Didn't even give her a name, for crying out loud!), God thought it'd be a great idea if Ruth takes a cup of water every time she visits a woman and starts her conversation with, 'This is a cup of the living water to refresh your soul"

SAUL: Saul spent most of his life on earth alone, tending his sheep, with very little company until Hannah and Ruth came into his life. Understandably, Saul remains on his initial vacation and has become quite a party animal in many of the Adventure Planets System. His guardian angel gets a bit frustrated, but God just laughs at the angel, "Ah leave 'em alone. The old man's having fun and I think it's great." God tells the angel.

Note To Readers

As I was thinking through the four children who would be recruited for the army of Hannah's Huggers, I started to think of names for them. I didn't want to just throw in four names. That's too simple. I wanted the names to mean something. It wasn't hard for me to decide, though. My daughter, Tracy, passed away from breast cancer 5 years ago at the age of 37. I wanted to honor the four people in my family's circle that have had to battle this dreadful disease, as a simple 'tip of the hat' for what they must endure. I ask all my readers to pray for them, and their families and continue to support those who suffer the loss of loved ones through cancer.

Sidebar: I did have to research the Muslim names for my last chapter (as well as many of the traditions I used in this book during the time of Jesus) because as a writer, even though it is fiction (sorry Chris) I never want to be too obvious that I have no idea what I'm talking about, even though most of the time that is the case. So I chose Fatima because the cyber world tells me that means 'Shining One' which seemed so appropriate and Abdul Raheem because cyber world tells me that stands for 'Servant of the Compassionate One' which fit the ending well, I thought.

For more info: Visit Tracy's facebook page, "It's Positively Cancer"

Or for the author: Visit www.TKRwriteNOW.com

9 780578 534527